The Sabre & the Shawl

Chanson, 3 January 1805

With a heavy heart, I must record that I am now certain that Therese
has established a new liaison – with Colonel Bertrand – a hussar. To
humour her, I am obliged to invite the man to be a guest at 'Chanson'.
All the signs were already there. In the week he has been under my roof,
they have magnified. The looks they exchange, the morning rides, the
disappearances from company – all of it is of the past pattern. She has
been quiet since the affair with Lieutenant Colonel Dupont, which cost
me a good sum to end, though I would have paid fourfold… Now we are
on the merry-go-round again. Do they think I am blind and deaf? Totally
obtuse? Perhaps they do not care that I know. Who can tell? Much is
clear enough, but much is also covered in doubt. If I fight a duel he will
kill me, just as his two predecessors would have… At least, the Emperor's
fortunes continue to rise, as does my own financial situation. This week a
new order for 5,000 light cavalry saddles – so perhaps my concern on the
drought in hostilities is about to end. I know this is a selfish viewpoint.

Anton Brun

Praise for Marshall Browne's writing

'In a market glutted with copycats, Marshall Browne is a refreshingly original voice' *Cleveland Plain Dealer*

'(His) highly individual style is painterly—not watercolours, but strong oils—and he has a precise eye for detail' *The Weekend Australian*

'Marshall Browne is an adroit storyteller … He is also a literate historian, which adds colour and authority to his intrigues' *Herald Sun*

'A great deal of style and imagination' *Chicago Tribune*

'Precise, efficient prose, colourful descriptions' *US Library Journal*

'Exquisite pacing and a finely-tuned sense of the unsettling' *Denver Rocky Mountain News*

'(His) style and the use of the English language … a joy to read' *The Examiner*

'Browne wrings exquisite tension from each subtly realized glance, thought, and hesitation … and his plot twists captivate without straining for effect' *Booklist*

'… brings alive the Nazi Regime and its evil as well as any book I have ever read' *Speaker Newt Gingrich*

'Like the shifting reality of Schmidt's life, the changes in his character are as subtle as they are harrowing, a triumph to Browne's clean, exacting style' *New York Times Book Review*

'Burningly brilliant … a page-turner novel. It's the best Australian book I've opened this year' *Adelaide Advertiser'*

'Browne is terrific at building character and setting scenes' *Minnesota Star Tribune*

'This elegant and intelligent mystery steadily draws the reader into its thrall … to a surprising and violent conclusion.' *Canberra Times*

'The sense of immediacy to Browne's writing, as well as the emotional richness of his characters, bolster this well-wrought story' *San Antonio Express-News*

'Utterly convincing evocation of a dread place and time, through characters that engage mind and heart. Brilliant storytelling.' *Kirkus Reviews*

'A perfect example of how a book can be both good for you and incredibly entertaining … literate, redemptive and historically insightful—not merely accurate. It is also as suspenseful as anything you'll read this year.' *The Flint Journal, Michigan*

By the author

The Iron Heart
The Eye of the Abyss
Rendezvous at Kamakura Inn

Inspector Anders Mysteries:
Inspector Anders and the Blood Vendetta
Inspector Anders and the Ship of Fools
The Wooden Leg of Inspector Anders

Melbourne Novels:
The Gilded Cage
The Burnt City
The Trumpeting Angel

Far East Thrillers:
Dragonstrike
City of Masks
Dark Harbour

Short Stories:
Point of Departure, Point of Return

The Sabre & the Shawl

A Romance

Marshall Browne

ARCADIA

First published 2013, by Australian Scholarly Publishing Pty Ltd
7 Lt Lothian St Nth, North Melbourne, Vic 3051   TEL: 03 9329 6963   FAX: 03 9329 5452
EMAIL: aspic@ozemail.com.au   WEB: scholarly.info

ISBN 978-1-925003-34-5

Design and typesetting Art Rowlands   *Printing and binding* BPA Group Pty Ltd

This book is typeset in Fairfeild 12pt

For Merell and Justine, on our
wonderful journey …

'I have neither tears for the past nor fears for the future.'
                                                        Montaigne

Pierre Brun, the historical novelist, gazed across Paris's Jardin des Plantes from the balcony of his top-floor apartment. His gaze was far-seeing, his mind not on the verdant scene. He was turning over a situation that had come to him in a curious, and surprising, way. It was just after 8 a.m., on a Tuesday in April, and the air being exhaled by the green lung on the other side of the street was tingling fresh, seeming to match the sense of discovery in the novelist.

Pierre has published ten novels (all set in Paris), which – with one exception – have been well received by the critics. They've not earned him much money, yet he lives in very comfortable circumstances. That fact has strong roots in this story; mid-list writers are a breed as remote from the likes of Dan Brown as Saturn is from Earth; that is another fact which, as the editor of a small literary magazine, I observe with sorrow. I should say that Pierre has not attempted a new novel for five years; the main reason for this veritable drought seems to be the premature, and tragic, death of his wife – and his responsibility for it.

Pierre inherited his wealth, as did his chain of forebears, from another Monsieur Brun, a successful leather-maker, saddler and harness-supplier to Napoleon Bonaparte's armies – a Burgundian, Anton Brun, whose dates were 1759–1820.

Pierre is fifty, a tall, lean, brown-eyed man, with a prominent scar on his forehead – the white tissue stands out against his olive complexion like the duelling scar of a 1920s German officer (which, of course, it is not). To some women, observant of him, it suggests that he's lived his life to a fuller extent than their other male companions, and is a turn-on. And certain women do talk about Pierre – about his past, his future. One of his short-term lovers told her friend that he was 'damaged goods' and should be steered clear of. Although there was something in what had been confided, the friend also understood that a vested interest was being promoted.

Thus, he does retain an occasional eye for women. His most recent liaison ended on a cold night in February, outside the opera house. The red-haired, vivacious investment banker had been as glad as he to conclude their three-month long affair. The break-up hadn't been scripted in either of their minds. She'd looked into his eyes, and ad-libbed her lines. They'd walked away in different directions, a parting sealed with the lightest of kisses. He'd thought: If only such farewells could always be so brief and uncomplicated! Later, he wondered if she'd lifted it from the plot of the opera (which had such a twist). Since then, as with his writing, he'd been lying fallow. The time between novels is the time devoted to his liaisons; once at work, he is as reclusive as a monk in a remote Bhuttanese monastery. In 1995, he'd been at such a place. Last week, a divorced woman in her forties, with startling green eyes, intimated that she was available, was waiting in the wings. She might have to wait. The rest of his life might. So it now appeared, though as yet nothing was certain.

What had presented itself to him last Tuesday had not been a dreamy feed-in from his unconscious, was more akin to a sharp tap on the shoulder. But, was it a drought-breaker? After his initial astonishment, Pierre was intrigued by what he'd uncovered. In an unexpected source, he'd stumbled upon material that, in itself, was a strange, mysterious narrative.

On this April morning, standing on his balcony, coffee cup now put aside, he asked the Jardin des Plantes: 'Could this be my new novel?' The only response was a puff of breeze, but the pristine air whispering into his face from the bucolic greenery did seem an encouraging overture. He had a pervasive sense that what he'd been absorbed in reading since last Tuesday would turn out to be far from the whole story; that convoluted months of research would be needed as he delved for its 'hidden depths' (a phrase he released on unwary interviewers). However, for Pierre the way into a story is a daunting challenge. He has an almost pathological fear of false starts that can keep him inert for months, or forever. And, he needs another of his tools: the ignition point.

I must rein myself in. 'And who the hell are you?', you might well ask. 'Editor of a small literary magazine, are you? So? Where's the fit?' In the responding silence, perhaps you might venture a guess: 'The typical omniscient narrator? A pushy know-all?' In each case, I hope not. I wish to be non-typical, and as unobtrusive as I can be; as unobtrusive as my small magazine. I admit that I feel an ownership of the story to come, which may impel an occasional intervention. 'Fatal to the narrative flow', you might sneer. Maybe. Anyway, this will be a difficult story to find, to construct – as to point of view, as to sequence, as to what to include/exclude – suffice to say, I'm a keen observer of Pierre Brun, a person whom he does not know at all. And, he is going to need all the help he can get – if he can be enticed into the project, and I don't yet know the answer to that. But now we should get on, or attempt to.

Pierre brought them home in a canvas carry-all. Here was the forerunner to that tap on the shoulder; the three bulky leather-bound volumes he'd found in the old-fashioned safe-custody locker at the Banque du Sud. A letter had arrived from the bank, notifying clients that the depositary was to close and their boxes should be transferred to another branch – or, failing that, cleared. The existence of the deposit box was news to Pierre. Though he'd no memory of it, he supposed that his long-deceased father had changed its ownership to his name. The bank clerk identified him, and left him alone.

The volumes, each embossed on the spine with the letters 'AB' and the numerals of years from 1805 to 1807, were in an iron box in the dingy, stale-aired vault (no wonder they were leaving); nothing else. 'AB' – Anton Brun – his great-great-grandfather. What had the old boy been up to here? That evening after dinner, in his study corner of the big salon, a cognac in hand, he opened the volume for 1805. In its faded, sloping script, he read the first entry:

'Chanson', 3 January 1805
With a heavy heart, I must record that I am now certain that Therese has established a new liaison – with Colonel Bertrand – a hussar. To humour her, I am obliged to invite the man to be a guest at 'Chanson'. All the signs were already there. In the week he has been under my roof, they have magnified. The looks they exchange, the morning rides, the disappearances from company – all of it is of the past pattern. She has been quiet since the affair with Lieutenant Colonel Dupont, which cost me a good sum to end, though I would have paid fourfold. Of course, her subsequent silences were a further painful cost. Now we are on the merry-go-round again. Do they think I am blind and deaf? Totally obtuse? Perhaps they do not care that I know. Who can tell? Much is clear enough, but much is also covered in doubt. If I fight a duel, he will kill me, just as his two predecessors would have. They might spare an apologetic shrug at my demise, murmur, 'C'est la guerre'. Fortunately, they have both fallen in the Emperor's service and lie mouldering in battlefield graves. It seems I am back to such a waiting game with Colonel Bertrand. These officers are like the brilliant-hued dragonflies humming over sun-warmed ponds at noon. It seems to me that their spans of existence are

similarly measured out. Though not all; some have great luck. However, the Grande Armée has not been to war for four years, which, in this current case of Bertrand, is a concern. Further, I sense that he might be a lucky one … At least, the Emperor's fortunes continue to rise, as does my own financial situation. This week, a new order for 5,000 light cavalry saddles – so perhaps my concern on the drought in hostilities is about to end. I know that this is a selfish viewpoint.

That first night when Pierre looked up from his reading, rubbing his eyes as though to check that the Paris of this April evening of the twenty-first century still existed, it was nearly 1 a.m. Already he was deep in the 1805 world of Anton Brun, his wife Therese, and the hussar colonel; caught up in the toils of the Napoleonic era, its society, politics, and military adventurism; caught up in what was shaping as an incandescent love affair, shot through with his forebear's cuckolding.

From Anton Brun's careful comments, it was clear that Therese had been a notable beauty, a passionate, tempestuous woman; in her eyes, her marriage to the saddle-maker, in 1801, had been one of convenience. This was soon quite plain to his forebear. She wasn't deceiving or conspiratorial; in the murky hotbed of Parisian society, her several affairs were quite public. Within eighteen months, Anton found that his rare appearances in her boudoir had ceased. Pierre decided that he wasn't a man to beg for favours; he was a man to settle down, and hope for better times.

The Empire was a stage crowded with colourful actors – in one entry, Monsieur Brun had selected the word 'infested' – thousands of officers of the Grande Armée, crowds of upwardly mobile officials, and the fortune-builders, like himself, of the mercantile classes studded into the mêlée, all awhirl as though at an exuberant and eternal grand ball. Amatory matters had a special cachet in this frenetic scene, and the quicksilver love affairs, and the gallant manoeuvres of the military men, in particular, in the salons and boudoirs, were legion. Anton Brun made that point.

Pierre, shoeless, padded through the apartment – 'lit like a stage-set', an actress lover had said – to make coffee. He wished to clear his head and press on. When he'd left 'Chanson', Anton had lived in this apartment for five years. Pierre knew that much. A good deal of his furniture and paintings remained *in situ*. He knew that, too, from his parents. The actress had described the apartment as opulent, though with a worn-at-the-edges character. She'd fixed Pierre with her mocking glance, as if the verdict was applicable to Pierre's character also; he only ever half-listened to that one's remarks, even in bed.

In an interview arranged by his publisher, he'd said that his ideas arose from the mists of his unconscious – by a mysterious transformation from a pot-pourri of past events, experiences, and impressions – laid down like wine. That was a bit rich; he was reluctant to talk about his processes; he never discussed tradecraft with other writers and nowadays avoided literary festivals. He'd heard too many train-wrecks of novelists spilling out their guts, on the bones and sinews and magical techniques behind their fictions. Best keep their mouths shut. His opinion.

He made coffee in the blazing white-tiled kitchen; that and the palatial bathroom were the only rooms modernised by his parents. Returning to the salon, the fragrance of the brew having its usual stimulatory effect on him, he sat down and took up the volume. He thought: Falling again into a lost world. But was anything ever lost? Certainly, he felt like he was stepping off a precipice into the story, as it unfolded in the restrained, yet semi-ironical tone that his forebear had perfected.

Between three and four o'clock, Pierre fell asleep in the armchair. After several hours in his bed, he breakfasted on the balcony, served by Madame Roget, a severe-faced woman from the area, who came in three days a week to housekeep and cook. Her husband is on cancer's dark road. She never refers to it; periodically he inquires, and receives a minimal reply. A dark road is a dark road. Meditatively sipping coffee, the two hundred-years-ago recorded incidents, events and opinions that he's read overnight sift in his mind; it occurs to him that they're also moving in the apartment at his back, in the currents of fresh air from the gardens, that the faded testimony is relishing its freedom after the two centuries of stale-aired neglect. He reviews each incident reported, each nuance of emotion, circulating – yes, he does feel it, like the draughts in the spacious rooms of 'Chanson'. He concludes that his forebear's introspective nature, lack of physical prowess, and the astonishing fecundity of the situation that he was enmeshed in, had frozen his willpower.

Pierre strokes his scar as if to smooth it down. There's no evidence – yet – that the saddle-maker resorted to drink, or a mistress's arms; a steadfast and almost inscrutable demeanour is maintained. Yet there is something going on between the lines, which Pierre wonders at but can't interpret. One might ask: invisible ink?

Staring into the coffee crystals, he divines: Yes, and something is going on in me. His imagination is rolling up its sleeves. At least, a preliminary canter. He smiles his lop-sided smile. 'Your non-committal grimace.' The actress's verdict, with malice. She's said it enough times for it to penetrate his non-listening mode. It had been an immense relief to show her the door. Politely. Gallantly. She'd had a lovely body, bathed in wonderful essences. For a time, each had masked her caustic wit.

Nonetheless, is Anton Brun the essence of his new novel?

At nine o'clock, walking in the gardens, his hat tilted over his eyes against the rising sun, his stick in hand, Pierre considered his forebear's situation in the year of 1805. Some men would have felt themselves in the eye of the storm; seemingly not Anton. Pierre frowned. Perhaps he'd been conditioned by the past episodes; perhaps, he thought again, his ironical nature, lack of physical prowess, and the astonishing power of this new affair had freeze-dried his resolve. So far. Pierre had read only into September 1805; the saddle-maker had not revealed any plan of action, or intention, to extricate them all from the contretemps. Surely, further reading would bring him to a watershed, though he doubted if Therese and the colonel saw a predicament at all.

Pierre paused to study a favourite plant. He could not name it. His late wife would have. She talked to the plants during their walks; he heard her low, affectionate voice right now. She was talking to him, too, he believed. Sun warmed the back of his hands. She would have loved this day – loved the natural world.

He turned to hurry back to Anton Brun, and 1805. Safer country than his own past; safer for his mental well-being.

In his salon, Pierre took up the volume and re-read an entry:

'Chanson', 17 February 1805
Tonight we went to Madame Latour's ball. At 10 p.m., I stand with Rey and Montmorency watching Therese whirling around the room in the arms of Bertrand – as they watch their wives in similar disport. Madame Rey is now attached to an officer of the Old Guard. The senior officers of that corps appear to be her abiding passion. Madame Montmorency has disappeared, possibly into the gardens, which will be very cold. Each of us is married to a lady of beauty – or, at least, style; ladies who, it seems, have unbridled passions. I stand in the mirrored, gilded room feeling myself an object of pity and ridicule. Our pride and the practicalities, however, do not permit us to share our common dilemma; we do pass brief, sympathetic glances between us, like the tiny cups of bitter black coffee being proffered by the servants. I suspect we each have a more intimate knowledge of the other's disaster than we do of our own. My notion of pity and ridicule, when I think of it, is irrelevant, made redundant by the fervour of the times. Regardless, I am glad to say that each of us maintains our dignity. Leaving the ball, alone, I note that a carriage drawn up in the drive is rocking in a violent motion. Then another. The coachmen are assembled near the gate chatting, and rubbing their hands against the cold.

Pierre turned pages, which felt glassy under his fingers, forward to September, and began to read from where he'd left off in the early hours. As the affair progressed, he read of known and suspected trysts. Therese had become a traveller to various destinations in France where her colonel was posted. Anton would stand on the terrace watching her carriage disappear down the drive to yet another rendezvous, his heart feeling as abraded as the crushed gravel under the revolving wheels; headed for a scented bed in some garrison town. He wrote: 'It appears that their appetite for each other is insatiable'. With one eye on the luminous affair, and the other on the storm clouds passing again over the Emperor's continent, he fervently and candidly hoped that a fresh tide of war would soon carry off the colonel. He pictured the shovels of earth being flung into a battlefield grave, onto the war-hardened face.

In that October of 1805, doubtless each member of the cuckolded cadre held the same hopes. But in abeyance, as the Grande Armée had not been at war for those four years, Pierre reflected. He was consulting reference books, side by side with the journal, his afternoon tea on the table beside him, ignored.

'Humph', from Madame Roget as she collected the untouched tray. Pierre read:

Therese returned unexpectedly this evening. The voices and the flurry of the servants running out was the first intimation I had of her arrival. She was assisted by her maid as she entered the hall. We embraced formally. At a glance, I took in her exhaustion. She was travel-stained; tears had streaked the dust on her face, and she was distracted, near to swooning. I motioned my butler to also assist her. She gasped, 'Bertrand has gone to war. The whole army is on the move.' It must be

Austria, as the Paris papers speculate, but she was too spent to say more. She had supper in her apartment with our son, who had his third birthday while she was away. The servants arranged a party which I attended for a short while. They look after the child with care and affection. I dined alone. The candle-light, playing its brilliant dance on the vast expanse of my mahogany table, put into my mind a picture of long columns of men marching across a night-landscape, punctuated with a myriad of flickering camp-fires resembling fireflies. So, Colonel Bertrand is about to practise his profession again. Is he marching towards his fate? I say 'colonel' but he has been promoted to brigadier-general, is now in command of a brigade of hussars. I noted this a few days ago in the Ministry's intelligence column of the *Moniteur*.

Pierre looked up. A child? The first time Anton had mentioned this. A son. He frowned. In that era, possibly, not so strange, as children of the wealthy were left in the care of nurse-maids. He rose from his chair, flexing his arms then stretching his legs. Madame Roget had left. He'd not asked for dinner to be prepared – decided to eat at a restaurant. Dusk was settling on the city, as the Emperor's strategy had settled on that long-ago autumnal October. A thought came: 'Chanson'? The house which Anton Brun obviously loved. Pierre was becoming intimate with it from the journal's references, but knew nothing of how his forebear had acquired it, what it looked like, or what had happened to it when the saddle-maker had moved to this apartment.

The library covered three walls of a smaller room off the

apartment's main salon. Pierre, on an impulse, entered the room – a rare occurrence; switching on the lights he regarded the walls of burnished, antique leather. Throughout his life he'd sporadically explored this trove, not consciously thinking of Anton Brun. It was just something that had come down in the family. His father had never looked at it, as far as he knew, and he remembered his mother complaining about the dusting. The red-haired investment banker had commented, 'There's money here'. His own library, with its bright dust jackets, was in a corner of the main salon … Now, it had a context. He recalled that the books were broadly shelved by subject, and religion was a major feature, which now seemed an enigma: Anton hadn't made a single reference to God in the journal. He had none of the saddle-maker's private papers, presuming any had survived. Only the journal. Could a text or a reference to 'Chanson' be buried in these inscrutable leather walls? He stared, but did not move. It struck him that there was a remarkable uniformity to the bindings in colouring, in their condition … The saddle-maker had had the library re-bound with his own product! He turned his head, recalling another large section devoted to architecture and moving to it, ran his eye along the gilt-lettered embossed spines, did not disbelieve it when 'Chanson' sprang out at his eyes.

An element in the interior of Pierre's writing life had clicked into place, an element which he would never reveal to another soul. How to say this? He has two what he calls 'princes', really, mentor-like images in both his real and his fiction-writing lives – though often they seem as one life to him. This one was the Prince of Co-incidence, stepping out of his shadowy alcove in the novelist's mind. We will hear of the other, later. Both, in the details of their physical appearance and dress, are vivid in his mind; sometimes more so than his characters.

Pierre eased the large, slim volume from its place, and sticky with its dust bore it out to the salon to his desk. He guessed that it was two hundred years since it'd been in someone's hands. In one track in his mind, the advent of the journal is taking on an atmosphere of predestination.

With care, he turns back the leather-covered boards. On the front page, the house's facade was before him. He gazes at it, remembering Anton's references to its effect as the beholder views it from the sweeping gravelled drive: 'Simple and elegant – like the finest of ladies: like Therese'. The vestiges of pink watercolour on the wall add even more refinement, in Pierre's eyes. The draughtsman was exacting. Rapt, the novelist reads of its construction, its apartments, its furniture and artworks, its offices – of the hundred-hectare park with its grassy woodlands, its lake … He turns to stare at several paintings in his salon. Here they are! From the phraseology, the saddle-maker had written the text, and in it was evident a passion to rival his love for Therese.

Dinner time. Deep in thought, Pierre puts on his hat, takes up his cane and goes out into the streets for the second time this day. He looks preoccupied and dapper, maintaining his image of the historical novelist abroad – not for others, for himself. He walks to a restaurant at the western end of Boulevard St-Germain, which he patronises. It's not crowded and he is shown to his preferred corner table. The waiters are elderly, long since Parisians but originally from the country. The dark-panelled wooden walls are lit by amber-coloured lights. There's no music, only comfortable sounds from the kitchen, low voices from the patrons and waiters, and small percussions from cutlery in motion.

He meditates on the glass of pinot noir poured from the half-bottle he's ordered; from Gevrey-Chambertin – the Emperor's favourite, he's learned today courtesy of his forebear, who'd stocked his cellar and treated his palate with it. And why not? It was from Burgundy, his birth-place; the first time Pierre's drunk it. The district's vineyards continue, as can be expected in his country; however, has the style of the wine changed over the two hundred years since the Emperor last tasted it? Since Anton Brun had? Interesting questions, but serving to postpone those in the forefront of his mind. His meal arrives: *piperade*.

Between thoughtfully masticated mouthfuls: Is this his new novel? What does he have so far? A fairly straightforward story of unbridled passion and cuckoldry, incandescent to him because of the family heritage and the discovery of the historic family trove. He is hooked by his discovery of Anton Brun's life. Yet, neither Therese, nor the brigadier-general, has come to life in his mind; the saddle-maker's cool prose seems to mitigate against it; they are puppets, he tells himself. But perhaps, there will be a cumulative effect in the revelation of their personas as the account progresses. At any rate, he decides he'll read on – really, is compelled to. Isn't that a good sign? But where are the turning points, the twists? Yet again, he senses hidden depths and his other 'prince' – that of Imagination – is thus far, absent from the scene.

He finishes his meal, forgoes dessert – a concession to his diabetes – drinks a final half-glass of the wine. Smoothly, with its subtle wood spices, it slips down his throat like an old experience being relived. He will keep all options open.

A shower drifts down on the light-glazed branches of the plane tree outside the restaurant's window; when it stops, he will leave. He feels a compulsion to hurry back from contemporary life, and re-enter the world of Anton Brun. 'Anton!', he says softly, as if to summon the saddle-maker to be ready for his return.

The next morning at eight o'clock, Pierre again took his breakfast on the balcony. He absorbed the watery sunshine, and languid breeze – almost as a mild antidote to the revelation that he'd read of last night, after returning from the restaurant. It wasn't a dramatic turning point in the narrative, nonetheless it could certainly be termed a twist, although, he reflected, it could equally be considered as predictable. The saddle-maker had taken it without evident distress; Pierre now judged that his forebear was composing his journal, in language and tone, as an officer might lay down smoke to hide his movements on the battlefield. But in itself this was a puzzle. From whom was he seeking concealment? Pierre judged that the journal was not intended for the eyes of his contemporaries. From himself, then?

Surely Anton's intellect was too organised for such denial?

'Chanson', 7 November 1805
Last night, Brigadier-General Bertrand returned from his service at the Emperor's latest triumph – the Battle of Ulm. This was two weeks after Therese's homecoming. From my study window, I spied his arrival. Instantly my heart was beating faster. He was

quite alone, in contrast to the exuberant escort of his hussars that attended his departures. He rode slowly up the misty drive in the dusk, shrouded in the dirty yellow cloak he wore when on campaign. The park was still, and steely grey as the etchings of it in the hall. Only the horse's hoofs on the gravel and its flaring breath punctuated the silence until a hullabaloo from my grooms arose, sending the household running out to the terrace. I hastened from my study to find Therese embracing the hero even as he was helped from his mount by my men. His left arm was bandaged and in a sling, and Therese was half-swooning over this circumstance; over his survival – whenever he is absent, she torments herself on that particular. I stood at the rear of the crowd, but his eyes found me and he sent me a peremptory nod, as if to confirm his continuance in our life. This is his eleventh sabre or musket wound. Privately, I consider him a human chopping-block. I read that General Ney has many more. Both horse and rider were disorderly in appearance and clearly exhausted. The Emperor is reported to say that after a victory we drink champagne to celebrate, after a defeat we drink it because we need it. For one reason or another Bertrand, as he was assisted away by my men, seemed in dire need of our famous wine; I ordered my butler to take a bottle to his rooms. I have concluded that for the active participant, the margin between victory and defeat appears very narrow indeed. Therese and her servants, one of whom is a nurse, excitedly trailed behind him. I did not see her again until after 10 p.m., when there was a knock at my study door and she entered. I was surprised because she never comes to this room. Then I was astonished to see that she held out a single, long-stemmed, white rose – doubtless from my hot-house. 'Monsieur Brun – Anton', she said in her quiet voice. 'I wish to tell you that I'm with child.' Then she gave me her loveliest smile, turned, and left. That was all. I may have said to her back: 'I see, my dear'. But perhaps I said it only in my head. I gazed at the rose in my hand. I heard today that poor Rey has died. A rare disease of the blood, they say, which probably means syphilis. Who would blame the poor fellow? The officers of the Old Guard will have an unimpeded run with Madame now – if they are risk-takers, and most of them are. A white rose? Does she mean it to symbolise a new life?

With child! Pierre sipped his black coffee, the strongest note in his morning, thus far. What had the saddle-maker's neighbours thought of the *ménage à trois* at 'Chanson'? He appeared to have only a circle of acquaintances, no close friends, no siblings or other family; at any rate, he mentioned no one. In response to his enquiry about her husband, Madame Roget replied, 'He is failing'. They have a nurse and she never asks for time off. Phlegmatic, Pierre thought. Or cold-hearted? Like his forebear? Though, as before, he sensed that a different heart than that was beating in the saddle-maker's breast.

So, if all went well, a bastard half-sibling to his son was going to appear. Pierre was almost tempted to look nine months ahead in the journal, but no, let it unfold. Until Bertrand, Therese's love affairs appeared to have shot across the firmament like meteors, to burn out as quickly when Anton brought his money into play. Instinctively, he felt that Anton had not made such an approach to the cavalry brigadier-general. He frowned; on another note, it seemed that his forebear was introducing nuances of corrosive wit into his entries. Was he penetrating the saddle-maker's smoke-screen?

At nine o'clock on this Wednesday morning, Pierre re-entered his salon and, sitting down in his armchair, took up the journal.

It was at once evident that Anton Brun, the devout patriot – because he was that as well as being a commercial main-chancer – had flung himself into his factory's manufacturing operations with renewed vigour, 'delivering the harnesses and saddles essential to the glory of the Empire' – the phrase fell under the novelist's eye. The Emperor had unfinished business with Austria. Pierre read on. Bertrand's wound was healing – it was a relatively light one. The surgeon came and went, as did the nurses, as did Therese from his rooms. The lovers ate together in Bertrand's sitting room; the saddle-maker graced his dining table in nightly solitude. Once he'd visited the brigadier-general's rooms to enquire after his health, and to give his respects, but the cavalryman had sent out his apologies; he could not see him. Brun walked away down his own corridor, feeling a stranger in his own house. For a day each week he visited his factory at Lille; he began to attend there more often. One morning, a hussar galloped up the drive with a dispatch: Bertrand was recalled to duty.

The telephone rang in the apartment's hall. Pierre lifted his eyes from the now so familiar script, needed a respite, he realised. He stood up, stretching his back. Madame Roget was taking a message. It was the green-eyed divorcee, checking his status. Unchanged. At a signal from him, his housekeeper gave an apology. Quite delicately done, he thought. He returned to his chair and Madame Roget brought a light luncheon of bread and cheese: a modest helping of cheddar. Whenever he looked at cheese, he remembered his diabetes.

For the rest of the afternoon, Pierre gave himself a break from the reading. His eyes were strained; he needed a new prescription for his spectacles. He meditated on the many questions that had begun to queue up in his mind. Why hadn't his forebear divorced his errant wife – pocketed his pride, if that was a pervasive factor, grasped the treacherous nettle and plucked it from the soil of his beloved 'Chanson'? No! At a deeper level, he'd sensed that such action was not in the saddle-maker's character; that the love for his wife was all-consuming, a force beyond even his passion for business, for leather. The journal touched on an early remonstration which was civilised, even restrained, as if a wayward climbing flower on a stone wall was being discussed. On the surface, but in being in each of them, a state of grace was maintained; Therese was as kind and considerate of him as her passion would allow.

In that November of 1805, in a rare confidential moment, when he'd discovered her alone with her embroidery, she'd said: 'My spirit, my whole being is consumed with this great love. Forgive me, my dear Anton.' Pierre concluded that he had, and did. It was the only other entry, hitherto, that he'd found where she'd mentioned the contretemps. Yet, it seemed to the novelist that its unspoken presence between them was as fixed in the landscape of their life as the oak trees studded into the grassy park of 'Chanson'. He remained, nonetheless, in search of the tormented soul, somewhere between the lines … in that invisible ink.

After all, Anton Brun was a human being!

What had Bertrand thought of his host, or had he thought of him at all? Had he considered him as one with the furniture and art objects of the lovely château, a mere pawn on the giant chessboard that overlaid the Continent, and the brigadier-general's life?

'Anton, I don't know where I am with you', Pierre muttered. Despite the various conclusions that he'd made thus far, the saddle-maker hovered in his mind, Sphinx-like. In Egypt, in July 1798, Bonaparte had gazed upon that vision, possibly with similar mystification, he thought.

Dinner. Madame Roget had prepared a *confit au canard* for him to heat up. He did so, drinking two glasses of a crisp, white Vouvray which he'd uncorked earlier in the week. He ate at the kitchen table in the glare of the white tiles, and thought he heard echoes of his parents' voices, though they'd been dead over twenty years. His late wife was a gourmet cook; he never heard echoes from her in the kitchen. Other places.

At 9 p.m., Pierre returned to the salon and took up the journal for 1806. In January, 'Chanson' was inundated with snow; his forebear had not referred to any Christmas festivities, had not made an entry on Christmas Day. Perhaps Therese, suffering from the cold, with her pregnancy advancing, had kept to her apartments with their child, dreaming of the absent Bertrand. He had taken part with his brigade in the battle of Austerlitz. The Emperor had soundly defeated the Austrians and the Russians, and a hussar, on the road for five days, had been despatched by the cavalryman to 'Chanson' to proclaim the victory. The aide-de-camp had arrived two days after the victory was announced in the *Moniteur*. The brigadier-general was unharmed. Anton wrote that evening: 'While walking my corridors today, I heard my dear wife singing'.

Pierre looks up from his reading; a sound in the interior. Whisperings and stirrings are commonplace in this old building, but each day now he feels himself tuning into them and other peripheral influences in his existence, just as he is to the margins of the saddle-maker's.

'Between the lines of the journal, off the edges of its pages', he murmurs.

Tonight, the apartment is shadowy and still; unseasonably humid. The garden across the street is relishing it, drinking in the moisture, sucking any breeze into its green lungs. The salon's windows stand open, but the huge curtains at their sides hang as rigid as steel plates from the high brass rods. In this atmosphere, Pierre feels his heart beating. He tells himself, 'I'm living in two worlds'. Yet the novel, also hovering at the periphery of his existence, refuses to put on weight in his mind, to reveal a direction. He is absorbed in collecting information, entering and exiting Napoleonic texts in tandem with the saddle-maker's dated entries. Sponge-like. Surely, something must come of this. Is his heart beating because he's panicking – at missing a vital element, the hidden depths of his forebear's narrative, at failing to find the ignition point?

He turns in his chair. A vase, as tall as he, stands twenty paces distant, luminous in the salon's dusk: a thing of beauty and mystery. Brought from China, his mother had said. It must have come under the eyes of Anton, Therese and Bertrand; must have been imported from a place well beyond the Emperor's most distant military forays. Brooding in the present moment, Pierre wonders if the glowing light from its incandescent glaze is signalling back to its old land.

Footfalls are in the interior, he senses rather than hears; vibrations, not of the physical world. Anton is on the move. He announces quietly: 'Welcome back'.

He lowers his eyes to 1806.

'Chanson', 5 January 1806

He has returned. Yesterday evening, muffled in the yellow cloak, he trotted up the drive on a grey horse attended by a single hussar who led spare horses. In a kind of vague anticipation that morning, I had the snow cleared from the drive. He was shaking with the chill, and moving as stiffly as a ramrod when I met him in the hall. I shook his hand, which was trembling. Despite all that is between us, his courage, and unstinting service to our country, should be acknowledged. He was weary beyond words, just touched me on the shoulder. Therese had run to his rooms to await him. I retired to my study, and sipped a cognac. In recent weeks, I have read in the newspapers of the glorious victory at Austerlitz. Perhaps Bertrand will give me close details, but that is doubtful. On the few occasions we have talked, he has not given me much about his war experiences. Therese sends out a few words by her personal maid: he has been granted a long furlough, and will be with us through the spring; for the arrival of her child, although she did not mention that.

Pierre read on into the early hours. The temperature became cooler. The traffic sounds of the city diminished to an occasional distant siren. At 3 a.m., he retired to his bed, an antique sledge-like affair, once owned by Anton: Had he ever slept in it? In his slumbers, he dreams of the three principal players in Anton's journal, tenuously picturing events ahead of his actual reading: speculative walks, rides, and drives down which the story of Therese, Bertrand and the saddle-maker might go in the coming spring.

That morning, the novelist slept in. It was nearly nine when he appeared on the balcony and peered over the botanical garden. A few moments later, Madame Roget came out with the coffee pot and his croissant – one only, his diabetic ration. He did not wish to look at her stern face this morning, or ask after her dying husband; his mind had abruptly fixed itself on the imperative of moving ahead into the journal at a much faster pace. He must know the totality of the story recorded therein by the saddle-maker, so that he can either plot the way forward into his novel, or abandon it.

For the next three days, he read throughout the day until late in each evening, taking aspirin to combat his eye-strain and headaches. Meal times were brief, his morning walks were abandoned, and the few contacts from the outside world by telephone and letter, put aside. The saddler-maker's voice became a mild-mannered yet persistent monologue in his brain.

In late April, 'Chanson' was awash with wildflowers waving in errant breezes, washed with passing showers, the oaks and plane trees filigreed with crisp new leaves. The saddle-maker took several long walks in his park, breathing in air as fresh and sensuous to him as the aroma from the sheets of newly tanned leather at Lille. Despite all, his life went on.

'Chanson', April 1806

Today, late in the morning, I walked to the lake, and fully around it. Earlier, Therese had waved to me as she and her brigadier-general cantered past on chestnut horses, coats shimmering from the hands of my grooms. They had passed out of sight. Later, following a curve of the lake I spied the two tethered horses, nibbling grass at the edge of a copse of beech trees. Apparently, my wife and Bertrand had entered the copse and were now invisible in its dense undergrowth. I skirted its edge. I stopped. Somewhere in the distance an axe had begun to chop into a tree. Thunk, thunk, it sounded. Usually, the silence of my estate is almost religious in its intensity. I am a great admirer of silence. Even with my son in residence, my household marinates in it. He is a quiet little fellow. The work of a great estate, however, must go on. Suddenly a new note: Bertrand's hoarse voice, quite close by, shouting incomprehensible words, like orders in the heat of battle, quickly followed by a flow of vibrating sobs from Therese. I walked on. A prickly woodland couch? They have the softest of beds in the château. Totally foreign to my life, my experience, the onset of their mercurial passion seems as unpredictable as a coastal wind gusting on-shore. In my mind, I do recall those lovely rippling undulations of her throat. It seems so long ago. I return to the terrace to take tea; to read the latest contract from the Ministry: carbine scabbards for the dragoons … I hope he is careful of her swollen belly.

Pierre smoothed the scar tissue on his forehead – a gesture almost of impatience, or frustration. His forebear had this amazing capacity to recover from episodes which would bring cold despair into any loving husband's heart, then to find shelter in subsequent pragmatic moments. 'Those lovely rippling undulations' spoke volumes. Pierre saw sunlight-dappled water in the phrase. He was surprised to read that Bertrand, on some nights, had begun to dine with the saddle-maker. Anton again recorded the soldier's brief touch to his shoulder on his return from Austerlitz. Pierre mused: reaching out from his exhaustion, almost a touch of affection. A conclusion that he felt certain his forebear would never have ventured to make, though it seemed to the novelist that in the notation there was a whiff of gratification. Pierre gazed at the written words. Good God! What did it mean?

Sitting either side of the saddle-maker's shimmering mahogany table, their faces marked by candle-light and shadows, they drank the Emperor's favourite wine – Bertrand would have no other pinot noir, although his attachment to cognac also showed great loyalty.

Therese was now very large and both day and evening rested in her apartment. Her morning ride in the park no longer eventuated, although Bertrand rode his grey stallion each day, in sunshine or rain. 'Exercising it for the next campaign', said the saddle-maker's head groom.

Their dinner conversations were spaced with long silences; wondering some more, Pierre deciphered: companionable silences. The brigadier-general had never married. The saddle-maker had made enquiries in that direction. He'd had many liaisons. There'd been a Polish countess, a rich Belgian widow. After dinner, the pair now quite often strolled on the terrace in the spring air, smoking cigars. Haltingly, Bertrand expounded his limited ideas on

26

politics, puzzled over what England was up to. He was most at home in speaking of the Emperor, in quoting the great man's maxims. A favourite: 'Charges of cavalry are equally useful at the beginning, the middle, and the end of a battle'. A simple guide for fire-branded cavalry officers. Also, on discussing points of cavalry equipment, even grandly deferring in this to his host. One evening he'd pronounced, 'My dear Brun, we are both at the cutting edge of a glorious epoch: me with my hussars, you with your saddles'.

'The whole of France is at the cutting edge', the saddle-maker later dourly recorded, adding, 'although, the fellow has more merit to him than I had previously thought'.

Standing up from his deep leather chair, Pierre stretches his arms and back. He's just read of an event which seems an appropriate juncture to take a break. Two things have happened … He looks around the salon, glassy-eyed, finds it's nearly 6 p.m. He's given no instructions for dinner. He hasn't left the apartment for three days – or is it four? God knows how much coffee he's drunk. Not good. Madame Roget, in her doom-like character, has brought trays of food to the table beside his chair, taken them away again, usually with her exclamation: 'Humph!'

He will go to the restaurant at the western end of the Boulevard St-Germain, drink the Emperor's wine. He hasn't shaved today; no matter, the restaurant's proprietor, Monsieur Jacques, is pleased to have the novelist as a patron, and tonight his unshaven appearance will have a literary cachet. He takes hat, stick, raincoat and ventures out to the streets. Rainy air. Droplets of water spot his face. He thinks: Anton must have felt the same on his face as he paced the terrace with the brigadier-general that spring of 1806.

Monsieur Jacques comes to the corner table to welcome him. His white face is shaved as smooth as a billiard ball. The proprietor appears only for special guests. Mainly he keeps to his half-lit cubby-hole of an office, sipping a cognac, and watching proceedings through a small window in the wainscoted wall. Gravely, he says, 'I trust you are in good health, and working well, maestro'. Pierre nods.

'I do recommend the *cassoulet*. Paul is cooking tonight.'

A bottle of the pinot noir is opened. Pierre studies the deep ruby colour in the glass, takes a sip. 'Generous and bright in the mouth, subtle wood spices and red fruits.' The Emperor, and the saddle-maker, knew what they were about.

Like the wine, he re-tastes Anton Brun's words read within the past hour:

Today the three colonels commanding the regiments of Bertrand's brigade came to 'Chanson' to confer with the general. Something is afoot. They remained closeted for three hours, hawk-like fellows in plain undress uniforms, all in their forties, I guessed, but with the air of veterans. At a casual glance, each one resembles the brigadier-general, as if struck from the same mould. There is nothing loose-limbed about them. Like clockwork figures, they stalked through my halls and corridors, doubtless stiff from their wounds and the rheumatism of exposure to all weathers. I sent in refreshments, including a crisp, cool Loire wine. They left in a carriage and, over dinner, he tells me he must return to duty in three days, gives no reason. The Emperor's future plans are strictly secret. This afternoon, Therese has taken to her bed and the château is filled with an atmosphere of expectation. The surgeon and midwife have been sent for. It will be a close-run thing if Bertrand is to be present for the birth.

These were the two developments which had given Pierre pause. He'd not yielded to the temptation to look ahead – wished the saddle-maker's narrative to roll upon him like the grey-caps surging in on Brittany's 'land of the sea', where he'd lived while writing two of his novels. At that time, it had struck him that those stories, with their complications and turning points, had streamed each night into his mind across the moonlit sands with the tide.

The *cassoulet* from the unseen Paul's hands was as tasty as usual, and putting his diabetes on hold Pierre ate a pastry for dessert, brought from the nearby Peltier shop. Monsieur Jacques popped out of his cubby-hole to wave him a farewell.

Last night, he'd had a nightmare. One that he hadn't had in a long time: the smoking wreck of the car, the wan, dead face beside him glittering with fragments of glass – the mesmerising shock. He'd started up in bed, staring into the darkness as he had so many nights in his bunk at the prison farm; then, the world of the saddle-maker flooded back, replacing his sad debris with its own.

Thank God. Now in the breezy street, he fingers the scar tissue on his brow.

At home, turning the reading lamp on, he sinks into his chair, takes up the journal and reads:

'Chanson', 20 June 1806

At 4.20 a.m., Therese was safely delivered of a daughter. For a half-hour, her cries pierced my heart as I waited in the corridor outside her apartment. After it was done, I walked out to the dark terrace. Bertrand's travelling baggage was stacked in the front hall. His grey stallion, held by a groom, saddled, was in the drive snorting and backing as if smelling a forthcoming battle. Bertrand was nowhere to be seen. I needed to calm myself. I breathed in the cool dawn air. Doves began to sound their soothing notes. I recalled the long-stemmed white rose held out to me in the door of my study, months ago, and another since then. I have tried to understand what they meant, but I do not. I heard the heavy tread of boots and the jingle of spurs behind me. At the same moment, a party of horsemen appeared in the drive two hundred metres distant and cantered towards the house. His escort: a troop of hussars, the horses' hooves pounding the gravel, the rising sun stabbing gleams of light from equipment, shouted orders cleaving the air. I turned to greet the brigadier-general. He clapped me on the shoulder, and seized my hand in his calloused own. 'You should have champagne', I breathed. 'When I return', he laughed, in high spirits. He went down the steps to mount the grey stallion, as the troop wheeled into line and the officers saluted.

Me again. It has been a while. I've been watching and waiting. At this juncture, I feel it necessary to step into the situation, in effect, to read over Pierre's shoulder. He has noted the significant change in the relations, in attitudes, between the two men, and it's puzzling him. As the meaning of the rose evades his forebear, the growing familiarity between the adversaries also seems a conundrum to him, although, describing Anton Brun as an adversary to the cavalry general perhaps mis-states the situation. Certainly, in matters of business he is an adversary to many, but in the field of personal relations, no.

At least the novelist is well-set in his journey into the saddle-maker's story, but he has reached no conclusion on whether it gives him his new novel. For me, this is a point of concern. He is an experienced writer, conditioned by creative difficulties, and they can be the hardest to motivate. He is expectant of developments that will unfold in the journal, but thus far, I must admit, the course of events has been fairly predictable. His Prince of Co-incidence has made a cameo appearance, but the Prince of Imagination is not yet in the picture. Like a good cocktail, the story needs a telling ingredient. So, what can be done?

As usual at this hour, 11 p.m., Pierre's salon is steeped in its shadows, the only illumination coming from the reading-lamp and the street-lighting. In this precinct, the city is quietening down, though the ubiquitous municipal sirens encroach, now and then, from an adjoining *arrondissement*. Pierre goes to the kitchen, brews a pot of coffee, carries it out to the balcony. He pours a cup and stands in contemplation of the Jardin des Plantes, which he's long felt guards his apartment's night-time silence. With his own addiction to silence, his forebear may – in his last years and with 'Chanson' just a dream – have stood here thinking something similar. Pierre would've given much to know this for sure, and his actual thoughts.

The novelist smells the greenery, the coffee fragrance, concentrates his mind; he must get forward in his quest.

Up to a point, the journal conveys the saddle-maker's thinking. But everything is 'up to a point', Pierre thinks. He's not deciphering the invisible ink; the dark tract in Anton Brun's mind that he senses exists, remains submerged; he imagines it as a limpid forest pool at midnight, flecked by moonlight. The fact is, the love of his wife's life comes and goes from their existence at the Emperor's dictates. Passion is put into abeyance for a new campaign, is renewed when the Emperor has achieved an objective. Unless the brigadier-general is killed, it seems that the game will continue in an identical pattern, and if he's killed it's the end of the story – isn't it?

This is no use to me, Pierre thinks. Should he telephone the green-eyed divorcee? Get on with his life? Maybe there is no dark tract, or invisible ink. Is his resolve petering out?

There are the children … perhaps there's a way forward in that direction. Pierre turns his head, apprehends that he may not be alone on the balcony, that his resolve is being nurtured.

This new morning, Madame Roget has allowed him two croissants and extra butter. How is her husband? A better night, she replies. Pierre has woken up with a new spirit of determination. A sunlit April morning. He is not done yet, he tells himself, relishing his breakfast. Back to the journal …

'Chanson', 30 June 1806

Early this morning, I went to Therese's apartments to enquire after her health. She is well and spoke to me from her bed, as I stood in the doorway. I told her the details of Bertrand's departure, and she heaved a tremulous sigh. The nurse held up the new child, showing it to my small son who gazed in wonder at his half-sister. I have postponed a visit to my factory at Lille. All is well in that direction. We do not know where Bertrand and his brigade are going and this morning's *Moniteur* has no detailed information. At noon, news came from a mutual acquaintance that poor Montmorency has taken to his bed and is not expected to leave it. His heart is failing. He always seemed in good health, and even in good, if fatalistic, spirits, as we drank our small cups of bitter coffee in the many salons and ballrooms where our wives disported. I regret his misfortune. He may have been a more sensitive soul than he showed. I suspect that his wife's infidelities with the officers of the Grande Armée have corroded that vital organ. Although I have no worrying intimations, I wonder at the condition of my own.

Pierre wonders at his health, too; on a few steep streets, he's noticed a slight shortage of breath. Apart from the effect on his eyes of his marathon read, he finds that his neck, shoulders and legs are frequently stiffening up. Each half-hour he rises from the chair and does stretching exercises. Rapidly he blinks his eyes to moisten them. He imagines his forebear had written these tomes by candle-light, or by lamp-light. If so, his eyes must have suffered.

Steadfastly he reads on. He has arrived at September

1806. Three months have passed since Bertrand rode off on the morning of his daughter's birth. Letters had arrived each week, but Anton wasn't privy to their contents. Therese does give him grains of information: he is well, he is in Hanover, the troops are in good spirits, the Prussian King is proving difficult and may need to be taught a lesson. Anton was surprised; in his ears, this kind of gossip from Bertrand seemed out of character; perhaps, he noted, he had always confided such to Therese.

During his brief breaks, Pierre has taken to studying the saddle-maker's paintings and etchings, and now he looks at an etching in the apartment's main hall. Dark and tragic. A French soldier is about to be beheaded by a mad-eyed Spanish peasant. Stomach-churning stuff. Abruptly, the novelist turns his back on the moment of terror frozen in the Frenchman's rolled-up eyes – mirrors of horror. With the dark clouds of Spain and Russia gathering over his future, it was tragic that the Emperor hadn't turned his back on that approaching weather; he was on a treadmill of politics and expediency, Pierre reflected; too many balls in the air.

Each morning, under the cascading warmth of the old rose-head shower, images and scenes from Anton Brun's pen fretted in his brain, like the sunlight playing on the terrace at 'Chanson' – so thought the novelist. Insights? Sometimes, nothing. But this morning, half-asleep under the warm flow, shafting into his mind: pay-dirt! A man at the far end of the terrace leans on the balustrade, his back turned to the watcher from the earthly plane. That familiar back! The broad, over-coated shoulders – as if he'd materialised from a winter season – the thick, black curls on the nape of his neck beneath the homburg; the mother-of-pearl inlaid stick, the cigar in his left hand; studying the view, analysing the possibilities of the situation. The image, to Pierre, of Orson Welles as he'd been in *The Third Man*.

Pierre stepped out of the shower, his heart beating a little faster. The game's afoot, he told himself. The Prince of Imagination had arrived, and the novelist knew that he would be on his side.

Back in his chair, back in the journal, Pierre read:

'Chanson', 14 October 1806

Paris is alive with speculation about an impending battle. The Emperor, according to reports in the *Moniteur*, has massed his armies in Prussia. Prussian officers are said to have been sharpening their swords on the steps of the French Embassy. I think they are overconfident fools. Bertrand's brigade must be there, however we have had no news for a fortnight. Therese asks me what the newspapers say; I am non-committal. Her nerves and sensibilities are frail and should not be unduly disturbed. I am to start a new collection. I have been considering it, and now I am decided. Throughout my life, I have assembled several disparate collections that are placed in rooms in the château's east wing. The most extensive and the closest to my heart, displayed in glass cases taking up a whole room, is the butterfly collection. Displayed for my eyes only, I have never shared these collections with persons other than servants going about their duties. When he is older, perhaps I will show them to my son. Therese looked once, but was uninterested. The new collection I am about to begin will be extremely private. I will keep it in a small locked room, in cupboards which will also be locked. For the first time, there is to be an

element of adventure – even danger – in my collecting.
No matter, with thousands dying regularly in the wars
that have swept the Continent these past years, the
hundreds of thousands in constant peril at the behest
of the Emperor, it is a trifling risk in my trifling life. I
am quite resolved … Not long ago, I overheard Therese
tell a visiting lady friend that I kill butterflies. She
sounded puzzled. There was no criticism in her voice,
just that puzzlement. There is not a gram of ill-will or
rancour in my wife for myself – for any human being – I
am convinced of that. In the broad world of violence
and military derring-do which we inhabit, perhaps she
wonders why I have not attempted to kill her lovers,
or even to shoot the plentiful game on my estate as
most other landowners do. I do not know how to load
a firearm. And I have no such inclinations. Of course
we have never discussed it, nonetheless she must have
heard of the merchant in Lyons who has killed two of
his wife's military lovers in duels. Apparently, he is a
wonderful marksman – at twenty paces with a pistol,
deadly. He practices many mornings in the woods
near his house. Servants suspend red apples on twine
at the duelling distance, and he never misses. It was
written in the Lyons paper that he sees the red apples
as the beating hearts of the detested officers. There is
a colonel of grenadiers, formerly in garrison in Lyons,
whose return he eagerly awaits. But the colonel is
assiduous in obtaining postings which keep him on the
move – and remote from Lyons. In certain circles, the
merchant is quite celebrated: Montmorency expressed
his admiration to me one night, over the bitter black
coffee, which possibly that night seemed less bitter,

more hopeful to him. My new collecting, when I begin it, will depend on the skill and nerve of Marcel, my trusted coachman. Fortunately, he is well supplied with both. Despite my resolve, my own nerve will be what is really put to the test.

After reading this, Pierre rose from his chair and went out on the terrace. He stood gazing down at the gardens, tracing the fingers of his right hand over the scar tissue. Had this legacy from the great tragedy in his own life, from his criminal negligence, become a kind of talisman for him? The thought came and went like a jumping fish in the stream of the other preoccupations. A dangerous collection? Marcel? Putting his skill and nerve to the test? Slowly, deliberately, as simmering milk comes to the boil, the novelist felt a new excitement rising in him. The prospect of a turning point! The invisible ink materialising, as if on the application of a chemical. Under the shower, in his mind, his mentor, the Prince of Imagination, had arrived – presaging this development – giving him at last an incident to work with. Was it that? It was a great temptation to skip ahead into the densely written pages.

John Fowles, the English novelist whom he admired, wrote of the genesis of *The French Lieutenant's Woman*. 'A woman stands at the end of a deserted quay and stares out to sea. That was all.' Fowles went on to say that the woman was in a static long-shot, with her back turned on the land; that such mythopoeic stills floated into his mind very often, and that he ignored them, since that was the best way of finding out whether they really were the door into a new world. Pierre's image that morning, at the end of the terrace, had been of the shade he called the 'Prince of

Imagination'. Not a character in the narrative, as in Fowles' case, not even having the pseudo-blood and sinew of such. An interventionist, a construct of his fiction-making, his half-awake dreaming, a mystery personage; though, quite possibly, the Orson Welles look-alike could be a character if he so chose.

Pierre shakes his head, very slowly; it is Sunday and he needs his lunch. He longs for his wife's speciality from her lovely hands: *agneau à la bretonne*, but that isn't obtainable, unlike the novel that he is striving to find and may find, if he is unflagging – and lucky. Madame Roget has a casserole waiting for him in the refrigerator; notwithstanding, he will go out. Monsieur Jacques is closed on Sundays; he has another place in mind. First, he will walk to the Jardin du Luxembourg, have an aperitif in a café and consider and try to understand the significance of the point that Anton Brun appears to have arrived at: the new collection; he's no doubt that it's a turning point.

It's noon when the novelist reaches the café. Crowded. He finds a table beneath chestnut trees. Earlier in the day, it showered; now the clouds have dispersed and sunlight penetrates the filigree of new leaves to make a fidgeting pattern on the marble-topped, brass-bound table, on the backs of his square-shaped hands and the gold wedding ring. In recent years, two lady friends have made cautious suggestions: it's an article which might be, perhaps should be, relegated to a drawer – to the past. But he will always wear it. He asks for a Dubonnet with a dash of soda, a twist of orange peel. He wears a panama, has chosen an ebony-handled stick. Today's lonely image – for himself.

He sips the drink, nudges his mind back into his forebear's territory. The collector; another dimension, quite common in that era. He recalls paintings of rooms, crowded with stuffed birds and animals contained within glass domes, heads mounted on walls. Big-game hunting could be dangerous, but Anton isn't a hunter. The saddle-maker lives in dramatic times, is inveigled in a situation in which some men would be consumed with angst and hatred. Dangerous emotions. But Anton isn't in their grip. Seemingly, he remains detached, extraordinarily passive.

Pierre frowns. Surely he can't be in denial about the fact that he is good and properly cuckolded. Then, there's that flicker of intimacy between the two men, which he's noted recently. On the saddle-maker's side: ambivalence?

The divorcee with the brilliant green eyes – though he's too far away to see them today – is sitting at a table ten paces distant, in a party of men and women. She sits in profile to Pierre, hasn't seen him. He nods to himself. If he is going to move around town like this, his quarantine will be imperfect. He has no doubt that if she sees him, she will appear at his table, the search-light eyes examining every gram of his condition. She's told him that she has a passion for historical novels. Newly found? She tosses her dark head, is certainly attractive. The actress had a greedy passion for expensive dining … long-established, and demanding. Instinctively, he feels that this isn't the case with the green-eyed one. Pierre will never skulk away from a confrontation, but he does depart with discretion.

He eats his roast lamb at a bistro. It's only vaguely reminiscent of his wife's speciality, but satisfactory. Walking home in the mellow sunlight, his mind returned to a recent entry: a gift had arrived at 'Chanson' from Brigadier-General Bertrand – a beautiful Belgian lace shawl that apparently he'd found in Hanover. The saddle-maker recorded his surprise at such a delicate confection falling under the cavalryman's eye. 'Very expensive', Therese's personal maid had said as she passed her employer in a corridor. His wife spent most of her time in her apartments these days, quite often with the children. Once or twice, she'd walked on the terrace when there was sunshine, and she'd showed the precious garment to her husband, giving him a shy look. Quietly, she said: 'Only a man of great taste would have found this'. Monsieur Brun had dwelt on the heartfelt confidence for the rest of the day, valuing it for its rarity. He thought: She spoke as if she were my sister.

To the novelist, Sunday nights often seemed 'dead' time. If he wasn't working, or socialising, he might watch television; however, the flat-screen had remained dark now for nearly a fortnight. He retired to his chair and opened the journal at 15 October 1806. Big battles have been fought in Prussia. Rumours of more battles are sloshing around Paris like the autumn rains in the city's gutters. Dispatches from the Emperor are expected. Looking at his Google-generated timeline, Pierre checked that the battlefields were Jena and Auerstedt, fought on the same day. Within the next few days, a hussar should come trotting up the drive with news of the great victories.

On Monday morning, Pierre awoke to the faint sounds of Madame Roget's activities in the kitchen. Under the shower, he wondered at his strict discipline of reading the journal in chronological sequence. To find his ignition point, to stimulate his creative juices, it might be more productive to skip ahead, searching for arresting incidents and turning points – presuming they were to be found – or even to read from the end and work back in time. No, yet again, he decided. In the protagonists' lives, he felt a quickening pulse – and in his own. Coffee on the balcony, back to one croissant; the gardens, lung-like, breathing out the crisp spring air in his direction, on his side, force-feeding him oxygen for his brain. He must return to his reading chair. Danger is in the air.

'Chanson', 15 October 1806
The household is in a high state of expectation. News from Prussia is expected hourly. Therese is prostrated in an agony of anxiety, as is customary on these occasions. Personally, I have no doubt that our mutual friend, the brigadier-general, will survive, so I am busy with preparations to commence my new collection. I have given Marcel his instructions. He left my study, a very stern and thoughtful expression on his face, and I expected that. I gave him money to purchase a brace of the best quality pistols. He signals that he is practised at using them, which makes me wonder about his youth. I have written of my butterfly collection, now complete, but not of my collection of seventy-four Sèvres clocks. No one knows, but I am superstitious. Seventy-four is the age I hope to live to. Not unreasonably ambitious, and yet a satisfactory age to achieve. Those collections are complete, and now a new one is to begin. Already the carpenters are at work on the cabinets, and the locksmiths. I have

been appalled to read that, on occasions, the corpses of our fallen heroes are pillaged of their decorations and valuables, before they can be recovered by their comrades from the battlefield. This is particularly so if nightfall is imminent. It is well known that many senior officers wear their best uniforms, and most conspicuous orders and medals, into battle. I surmise that vanity is at play here: it is said by some that, in pursuit of additional honours and rewards, they wish to make their gallant acts of bravery and leadership more noticeable to the marshals – even to the Emperor! More charitable souls describe it as a means of encouraging their soldiers, or as a rallying point. Thus, stealthy and swift criminals are often able to harvest a bounty. Famous generals, especially if wounded, are usually borne from the field by their staff immediately they are struck. This is not always practicable. Montmorency, who is now on the verge of expiring, I heard today, made a special study of this, in following the movements of his wife's numerous lovers. In his view, it is the lesser generals and colonels who are the usual victims of such pillage. So, accompanied by Marcel, I plan to be present at whatever battles I can reach, to be on the scene immediately the tide of action has raced on; to pre-empt the villainous scavengers. I am still arranging other details of this plan in my mind, ones that are the most significant … I have been interrupted in my writing. A hussar has arrived. Bertrand is alive and will be home within a week. He has lost his left arm.

I intrude again – really, I'm always present, though in the background. I will be brief. Pierre is becoming absorbed in the saddle-maker's story (which is excellent news; as editors of literary magazines frequently do, I was beginning to despair). Each day, he is more and more intrigued by the subtle revelations from his forebear: the snippets of new information appearing in the journal entries, for instance; the apparent sea-change in the relationship between the two men – the growing ambivalence in Anton Brun towards the brigadier-general. 'Mutual friend' and 'home' illustrate this as well as the dinner talk, though minimal, which in recent months has broken the former sterile silences between them. It seems to Pierre that his forebear's brown-inked script is now more forthcoming. He still clings to his notion that Monsieur Brun has a hidden depth not yet visible, that there is invisible ink between the lines which will unlock mysterious aspects of his character; that it will give him his ignition point – another quaint notion of his. Other things are on his mind: surprise and puzzlement at the bizarre new collection – although, as he will discover, its conception is considerably more bizarre than yet revealed. I'd best let him get on with it. I believe that this novelist is now well-set in a course towards his new novel – barring accidents, and with judicious help from his mentors.

Pierre puts the journal aside and stands up. He feels in need of a glass of good pinot noir. Perhaps champagne would be more appropriate, in tribute to the Emperor's victory at Jena. Historians have judged it his most famous. But no, he opens a bottle of the Chambertin, pours a glass and carries it out to the balcony. The breeze on his face from the gardens is refreshing; mentally, he's named it the 'breeze of new discoveries'. On the balcony, Madame Roget is setting the luncheon table. She is serving the casserole which has been in waiting in the refrigerator. *Poulet breton*, a dish discovered during his novel-writing sojourn in Brittany. She hasn't consulted him; it is what he is having. His blood-sugar level will be on the rise; his depression, however, is on the wane. Take your pick, he thinks.

He sips wine. And, take your pick of which strand of Anton's narrative to follow. The tone of the journal has become quite conversational – the saddle-maker in dialogue with himself. Pierre frowns, concentrating. Is his notion that hidden depths lurk in the journal, in Anton Brun, a fallacy? He feels certain that his forebear didn't intend his journal to be read by his contemporaries. So why conceal anything? But, perhaps certain matters in his make-up lie latent, obscure even to himself.

Madame Roget serves his lunch. He sits at the table, studies the food. With a surge of warmth not entirely engendered by the wine, he tells himself: All is going to be revealed. Madame Roget pours him a second small glass. 'Monsieur?', he enquires. 'A good night', she replies.

That is good. He eats with relish. Bertrand has lost an arm. Surely it means the end to his career. The brace of fine pistols to be acquired by Marcel – what does that signify? He can't believe that the saddle-maker is to seek instruction in the art of duelling. So? He takes his coffee to the balcony rail and stares down into the street.

The green-eyed divorcee is below, standing next to the railings of the Jardin des Plantes, gazing up at him. The pale oval face is clear and cool beneath a stylish straw hat. She is absolutely still – as though viewing a wary animal in darkest

Africa – the thought wings into his startled mind. Then her lips move efficiently, and he reads the silent words: I saw you, yesterday. She raises a green parasol waves it at him, turns, and departs.

He stares after her. Had she come here on purpose or just been passing by? Good God, he's not yet certain of his novel, let alone begun the slog of writing it. He wonders if she will have that kind of endurance. Somehow, he must put this situation to rights. He senses urgency – an unease that if he doesn't do it, regrets will be in the offing.

'Chanson', 7 November 1806

Last night, at 8.15 p.m., Brigadier-General Bertrand arrived home. He came in a carriage, hussars riding behind leading his three mounts; the grey stallion is no longer in evidence. He was greatly fatigued by the journey and in pain from his wound. The bandage was bloody. He leant on Therese as they went to his rooms. He nodded to me in passing and I raised my hand in greeting. In addition to the loss of his hand and forearm, he is a wasted figure, must surely be headed for the retired list. I have sent an urgent summons to my surgeon. I went to my study to read the *Moniteur*. Its columns are crowded with reports of the recent battles; however, I am searching for intelligence of those that may come. I must keep abreast of all the political and military news in order to plan my new collection. Marcel has selected a light but sturdy landau for our forthcoming travels; also he has chosen Holsteiner bay horses. He claims that they are fast and strong and of good character. He showed me the pistols he has acquired. He said that they are the model issued to our dragoons. I have had bags packed with all necessary items. Our departure will be at short notice; the Emperor's plans are kept secret until the last. All collections should have a precise focus and I have given thought to this, although I believe that what I have decided was in my mind from the first. Assisted by an agent in Paris, who has been helpful in matters of commercial research, I have established a list of thirteen officers who were, or are, the lovers of the wives of Messieurs Rey and Montmorency, and of my dear Therese. Of the thirteen, four have died in action or of wounds, one has retired, and one expired from a rare blood disease – doubtless, a syphilitic scoundrel. My list is thus confined to seven serving officers. I am resigned to the fact that it will be like looking for a needle in a haystack. My Paris agent, nonetheless, is assiduous, and I'm sure will keep me informed on the movements of this group to the best of his ability. A large order for saddles and other equipment has been received – the largest ever. It seems that the Emperor does not intend to give our nation a respite from war. I am fortunate that he pays his military accounts with commendable promptitude.

Pierre stood up, stretched his back, rubbed his eyes, and began to pace the salon. Madame Roget had opened the windows wide, and the sultry spring afternoon air wafted in. Finally, he paused at a window and gazed up at the sky. He'd been startled, even disturbed, by what he'd just read – a sharper insight into his forebear's character! His pious words, about saving the insignia of fallen heroes from the human ravens of the battlefield, was a sham.

His prime motive, against those who'd cuckolded himself and his acquaintances, was revenge! How else could it be interpreted? And, he planned to keep the orders and medals for himself!

Yet, it was a twist to the saddle-maker's character that had possibilities for the novel, which he was now ninety per cent sure he would write.

Pierre needed a cognac and he went to the kitchen and poured a stiff one.

He returned to his reading chair, and plunged back into the saddle-maker's life and times. Dusk settled on the city, Madame Roget closed most of the windows, then departed, telling him of the dinner she'd left in the refrigerator; the birds in the gardens began their pre-nocturnal chirping, as the novelist steadily turned pages. Anton Brun did not write in his journal every day, but the time-gap until the end of November was unusual. Pierre wondered at it.

'Chanson', 30 November 1806
I have been indisposed this past week with a head-cold and kept to my rooms, eating little more than the chicken and rice broth that my cook, a good woman from Bordeaux, insisted I take as medicine. My surgeon has been attending to Bertrand's dressing each day and he has not left his apartments – until tonight, when we met for dinner. Therese has been coming and going from his rooms, and on one occasion I observed her carry their child in. I was eager to hear details of the two recent battles, and of the circumstances of his wounding. As usual, at dinner, the table and the room were illuminated by candle-light. The brigadier-general sat opposite me. He had a frail and ghostly appearance

and his voice was weak. He wore an undress uniform with no insignia. The servant cut his meal into small pieces so that he could manage to eat, although on one occasion, I rose and went around the table to make some finer cuts. I was pleased to note that he had no trouble with his glass and drank four glasses of Chambertin. He received his wound at Jena, in one of the cavalry charges led by Marshal Murat. A Prussian trooper sliced off his arm with a single slash. Almost at the same moment, the grey stallion was killed by a cannon ball. 'A noble animal', he murmured, 'a noble death'. He was too exhausted to engage in further talk. Obviously, the hour we had spent at table, and doubtless the wine, had wearied him. I suggested that he retire to his rooms. A servant waited to assist him, but he leaned on my arm as I saw him to his door. I believe that Therese is shocked at his condition, but overjoyed that he is alive and will be at 'Chanson' for a considerable time. I returned to my study; a letter from my agent in Paris awaits my attention.

Pierre read on. During the first weeks of December, Bertrand's convalescence continued and he regained some of his strength. However, Monsieur Brun pondered on his mental state. The brigadier-general sat for long hours in the library, sipping cognac, and brooding on matters indeterminate to the saddle-maker. Though he'd not yet viewed the carnage and horror of a battlefield, the owner of 'Chanson' imagined that such scenes were responsible for his guest's dark moods, and withdrawal from converse. The loss of so many of his men ... One night, he said, 'The best are gone, Monsieur. They cannot be replaced.' The saddle-maker reasoned that the damage to the brigadier-general's body now might extend to his mind, that the dozen bodily wounds were insignificant against the multitude of blood-stained images in his brain. This notion was reinforced one evening when Bertrand again appeared at the dinner table. The soldier had never been one for conversation, but he was now, at least, making brief declarative statements, as if impelled by an inner fire.

Pierre, massaging his scar, concluded that the cavalryman was trying to give tit-bits of information to his host, which might be of interest, or use. For instance, he'd said with a meaning glance, 'We took 40,000 horses from Prussia'.

One chilly December night, Bertrand insisted that they take a turn on the terrace. The saddle-maker was concerned for his guest's health; however, Bernard was not to be denied. On an apparent whim, he'd dressed for dinner in a splendid hussar gold-braided uniform with numerous orders and decorations – which doubtless attracted his host's close attention, Pierre surmised – and wore his brass-hilted, curved hussar sabre. It had been pointed out to his employer by Marcel that the weapon was of the plain, undecorated type, issued to troopers. All of this finery glittered in the candle-light. Though his walk remained far from steady, the brigadier-general no longer leaned on his host's arm. On this occasion, he'd walked ahead, muttering to himself and animated in a way that Anton had not previously observed. Suddenly, he'd turned, drawn the sabre from its scabbard, shouted '*Vive l'Empereur!*' and swept the weapon down in a ferocious cut. The saddle-maker sprang back, later reflecting in the journal that the whistling sound of displaced air might well have been the last sound an enemy, in single combat, heard. A last sound that he'd nearly made his own! In the dusk of the terrace, Anton heeded the burning light in the man's eyes. Rooted to the stone paving, he'd wondered if Bertrand had lost his sanity. Throughout the grey days, when not in his rooms or the library, the cavalry general stalked through the château's salons and corridors as though following a fitness regime, or a route that might take him to a calmer domain.

Anton concluded that his guest, though he'd not spoken of his future plans, had not abandoned hope of further service, which made the saddle-maker thoughtful. He'd begun to consider whether a leather fitment could be devised for the now white-boned stump, which might enable him to control a mount, leaving his right arm free for his sabre. He made a special trip to Lille to discuss it with his people.

Another Tuesday. It was three weeks since Pierre had disinterred the volumes from the bank vault. His eye-strain testified to it, and now he blinked several times to moisten them. He laid aside the journal for 1806. At 'Chanson', from the saddle-maker's perspective, Christmas hadn't been a joyous occasion. On Christmas Day, light snow fell and his forebear put on boots to walk around the semi-frozen lake, thinking that the children on the estate would soon be skating on it. Therese's world, now that winter had come, was confined to her apartments, with the children. Apparently, the brigadier-general took tea with her each day at 3 p.m.; probably a drear occasion, given the cavalryman's deep melancholia. Thank heavens, Anton recorded, he had his business to attend to; most days a courier arrived with papers and drawings from Lille. At the Emperor's direction, a carbine scabbard for the hussar regiments was to be manufactured.

Pierre went to the kitchen at 10.35 p.m. to have his dinner – a grilled pork chop with apple sauce, sauté potato and green beans – that he re-heated in the microwave. He ate with appetite, and drank a glass of the opened Chambertin. He was a man of only middle-age but he was living with ghosts. Anton Brun had admitted to being superstitious; Pierre was not, but he was religious, though a rare attendee at Mass. He believed that his deceased loved ones, and forebears, were always close by; that his dear lost wife was only a failed heart-beat away from him. He was convinced that one or another of them was often present, especially at dawn and dusk, with the breezes sighing into his apartment …

Perhaps due to the late dinner, he didn't sleep well. He awoke out of a nightmare that left no trace in his memory, as if retiring to re-group for another sortie. Re-grouping, as Bertrand's brigade was after Jena and Auerstedt, he reflected, lying in the dark in his forebear's sledge-bed. The colonels who'd first visited 'Chanson' had been killed, the brigadier-general told the saddle-maker; he'd enumerated the considerable losses of officers and men during Marshal Murat's frequent extravagant charges at those battles. He had not criticised the marshal; it was the nuts and bolts, the give and take of the chaos of combat, he inferred.

The rose-head shower's warm water was a restorative – necessary this morning. Vigorously he rubbed his chest and shoulders. As if in response, words which his forebear wrote in that new year of 1807 came into his head: 'Each morning, bright or dull, my beloved château sings to me. Even when I am far from home, it is a song in my heart.'

Water streaming from his head, Pierre wondered afresh at this poetic confidence from Anton; in setting this down, had the saddle-maker Brun also been in wonder at it?

'Chemotherapy again', Madame Roget responded to his enquiry, as she poured his coffee. Not such bad news, he knew. Her husband had had several courses, which were buying him time. He ate his croissant with berry jam. Yesterday his publisher had left a message, asking him to phone at his convenience. They'd not spoken for six months, might not for another, the way he was going.

What had been the fate of 'Chanson'? He'd phoned a real estate agent he knew to try to find out what had happened to the estate. He had no address as such, just the name of the nearest town; in its day, it must have been a local landmark. He'd searched via Google, without result.

He rose from the breakfast table, went to the balcony rail, saying in his head his wife's name, as he often did when confronting literary work: a mantra. He imagined, liked to think, that the leafy inhabitants of the Jardin des Plantes, beloved by his wife, were sending up greetings. In an unguarded moment – he didn't have many – he'd told the actress this. He'd been turned off by her derisive laugh; one of the multiple beginnings of the end, with her. For a while, her sumptuous, scented body had saved her. History.

The point he'd reached last night in the sledge-bed, before he'd dropped off, came winging back. The saddle-maker's next moves were sketched out, yet veiled by the mists of the French winter. A sinister expectancy hung over the planned new collection, and its apparent danger. Also, its practicality: the historical record showed that the Battle of Eylau, on 8 February, might be an opportunity. But the next was not until 14 June, the Battle of Friedland, and both in distant East Prussia. Would Anton and Marcel be able to get to such locations?

An apparent flaw in his forebear's character had surfaced – grist to the fictional mill?

One way or another, Brigadier-General Bertrand's days appeared numbered. Anton expressed his fear that the first chill to the cavalryman's chest would carry him off like an old man; yet he was barely fifty. And 'fear' was the operative word; the saddle-maker's ambivalent attitude towards the man who'd cuckolded him, who'd covered his wife to produce a child, was remarkable, spell-binding, Pierre concluded. And Therese? She was drifting through this story like a wraith, which, given her passionate nature, was a paradox.

Pierre savoured the coffee, sucked in oxygen. His pre-slumber thoughts last night were not the half of it. In his previous novels, he'd felt himself to be a character moving side-by-side with his fictional creations, part of their lives, brushing up against them in the street, in restaurants, overhearing their conversations, covertly glimpsing their facial expressions and gestures. In this case, the saddle-maker was centre stage, his mainstream thoughts and tribulations in brown-inked evidence; bit by bit, new facets of him were catching the light.

But he wasn't privy to Therese's inner life, nor the general's; he would need to summon the Prince of Imagination here. Though there must've been a stream of letters between them. Anton mentioned letters. Had any survived? He pondered other possibilities. The saddle-maker might have left a personal and business archive. For instance, in an institution at Lille, or held by a relative unknown to Pierre. The novelist had no siblings; nonetheless, there might be cousins somewhere, though most likely any papers had been destroyed on decease, as so many were in those days, he knew. At any rate, he would defer consideration of such matters until he had finished reading the journal. By then, much now clouded might have become clear.

Still he resisted skipping ahead in the journal, sensing that it was imperative to his understanding of the story, and absorption for his novel, that it came to him in its measured order, in the sober sentences of his forebear. Prince of Imagination? Why 'prince', why not 'king', or 'duke', or 'count'? No reason. The title chosen was the first that'd come to mind on a day of too much wine. Nomenclature was of no account; it was the subtle and fruitful prompting of this mentor, resident in his unconscious, that counted.

Pierre grimaced his actress-derided grin – 'Are you in pain?' – turned away from the greenery. Back to his reading chair.

'Chanson', 4 January 1807
I am concerned for Therese's health. On the two occasions I have seen her since Christmas, she has appeared even paler than usual, and certainly she is thinner. In the wretchedly cold month just past, she has kept to her apartments. Fires burn there day and night, as they do in all the château's main rooms, and it is wise for her, and the children, to stay in the even warmth. The thick drapes in her rooms exclude the draughts prevalent in other areas of the house. I have checked with my people: there is no shortage of logs for the fires. I have persuaded our guest to also keep

to his rooms. His earlier perambulations through the halls and corridors, thank heavens, have ceased. He is reading books from my library, including my history of 'Chanson'. Last night, for the first time, he invited me to take wine with him. I brought samples of new-tanned leather to show him. They had arrived that day from Lille, for my approval. We each sniffed at the rough-buffed products. The strong odour is nectar to me, and I believe also to him. I detected a slight relaxation in his stern visage, when he said, 'Very satisfactory, Monsieur, although I prefer the aroma of cognac'. I could not restrain my smile, and he looked away into the fire, a twitch of one on his own lips. The product is to be used for the manufacture of the large order of carbine scabbards, which are to be issued to many regiments of the light cavalry. Thus, I knew it would be of interest to him. An urgent delivery letter has arrived from my Paris agent. His intelligence is that the Grande Armée is concentrating in East Prussia, and that hostilities are imminent. I will consult Marcel and make my plans within the next day or two. Once again, the Emperor is on the move! But, I fear and hope, not Brigadier-General Bertrand.

'My history of 'Chanson'.' The cavalryman had held, in his remaining hand, the volume now present and correct on Pierre's desk. He finds this a warm and connective thought. Perhaps modern technology could detect Bertrand's fingerprints! The novelist, each day, is open to such small illuminations that he readily acknowledges are often byways to a dead-end; however, he feels confident that he is going to learn more about 'Chanson'. The saddle-maker wrote in the book's introduction that he'd acquired the château in 1785 from a bankrupt nobleman … Pierre puts the journal aside, and consults an article he's down-loaded from the internet on the Battle of Eylau. The saddle-maker had recorded 'East Prussia', and the web's time-line for 1807 indicated the next major battlefield as Eylau.

For an hour, he is absorbed in eye-witness accounts from men lost in that frozen landscape, in blinding snowstorms; he reads of blood-stained snow, frozen corpses of men and horses, the pitiful injured. Thirty thousand men dead and wounded! – a black, freezing, vision-impaired purgatory. It was said that the Emperor spent the following eight days criss-crossing the battlefield, until all the wounded of both sides were brought in. Apparently, on this occasion, he was dumbfounded by the butchery.

But it is still to come in the saddle-maker's journal, his life. Pierre thinks that his forebear and the trusty Marcel could never endure such catastrophic weather. It's a mission that will be aborted. He stands up, stretching his body then rubbing the back of his neck. A massage would work wonders; the red-headed investment banker had massages in her repertoire, and he misses them.

Another day without a shave, and without lunch; Madame Roget had grumbled, and he'd told her that he'd eat out tonight; she could rest assured. Given her husband's deadly situation, he wondered how she could worry about her employer's welfare. Notwithstanding her severity toward him, he'd realised, some time ago, that she did. He surmised that she saw him as both *enfant terrible* and helpless widower. Tonight, he'd again patronise Monsieur Jacques' restaurant, donate his unshaven literary aura to the establishment. After the horrific reports of Eylau, he needed several glasses of Chambertin. How the starving men on that battlefield must have hungered for food, wine and warmth; must have craved it, in the hours before they were blown apart, cut down, or died of exposure. He imagined that he'd be leading a legion of ghosts down the Boulevard St-Germain.

The telephone was ringing.

Monsieur Jacques, a whiff of cognac on his breath, led Pierre to the corner table, greeting him with: 'Your work goes well, I trust, maestro?' Pierre nodded. It was early and no other patrons had arrived. The proprietor fetched and uncorked the Chambertin himself, sniffed the cork, and poured a little into Pierre's glass. He arched an eyebrow on his billiard-ball-smooth face. 'Monsieur, perhaps we'll let it breathe a little?'

'Not necessary', Pierre said. 'Will you join me in a glass?'

This was unusual, but Monsieur Jacques did not show it. 'My pleasure, Monsieur.'

He brought another glass and filled both. 'I wish to drink a toast', Pierre said. He rose to stand beside the proprietor, and lifted his glass to eye-level. 'To the fallen at the Battle of Eylau!' The slight Jacques, immaculate in a veteran dinner-suit, repeated the words and they drank.

Pierre resumed his seat, thinking: The Emperor's favourite wine.

With a slight bow, his brown face still expressionless, Monsieur Jacques politely withdrew to his office, to be replaced by one of his aged retainers.

The crisp, spring evening is ideal for the *confit au canard*, which comes direct from its fragrant stove-top simmering, under the expert ministration of the invaluable Paul. Pierre ate slowly, brooding on the panelled, amber-lit walls but seeing – as if it were projected on the dark-stained timber – the freezing, homicidal, grey-toned landscape, with its multitude of deadly actors moving in wind-driven clouds of rain. Yes, ghosts. The Emperor had had trouble in getting the scenes at Eylau out of his head, as did Pierre on this spring evening two hundred years later. And the novelist had only read of them!

He eats camembert as dessert, from the department of Orne in Normandy, drinks a third glass of the pinot noir. The Emperor wrote six letters to Josephine in the aftermath of the battle – letters expressing his horror at the scenes he'd witnessed. Pierre speculated that perhaps, by this time, the great man's dreams were becoming populated by the shades of the million Frenchmen whose bodies mouldered in graves across the Continent.

The telephone call had been from his real estate acquaintance. He'd found 'Chanson'. It was about sixty kilometres north-east of Paris, on the road to Reims; the man drove up to see it. The château was a semi-ruin; a long time ago, a wing had been partially destroyed by fire; the windows were boarded up, the park and lake gone. It now sat on about a hectare of land surrounded by a 1970s housing estate. It was owned by a trust in Reims. He gave the information point-blank, did not think that Pierre would have the slightest interest in buying. Pierre hung up the phone, feeling a sharp disappointment. What else could he have expected? That the château still stood, given the surrounding development, was surprising.

Standing in his hall, he decided that he'd not go to see it. He didn't want to replace in his mind the saddle-maker's 'song' with a ruin. He'd shaken his head. 'The song has ended', he'd said aloud, bringing the vigilant Madame Roget out from the kitchen.

Finishing the cheese – the elderly waiter would be affronted if he didn't – he thought: One thing is certain; in that weather, Anton and his Marcel didn't make it to East Prussia.

As he walked home through the glitz and vibrant traffic of the Left Bank, the battlefield faded to the back of his mind. He'd not yet written a single note on his novel. He was taking a leap of faith that what he was reading, what he was thinking, was soaking into his unconscious, would reappear when needed in a refined form; that the Prince of Imagination, with his cynical eye, was already doing a cull.

'Chanson', 29 January 1807
Last night at dinner time, a courier arrived from my agent in Paris. It appears obvious that hostilities in East Prussia are imminent. News came, also, that two colonels of regiments of the line known to me, and well known to the late Monsieur Rey and Monsieur Montmorency, will be engaged in this campaign. The colonels are good friends – and almost brothers in appearance. I recall them walking arm-in-arm on a terrace at a ball we attended two years ago; the degree of similarity, and familiarity between them, in fact, was quite startling. To myself, I called them Tweedledum and Tweedledee – a note of humour, to lighten a situation which was not humorous at all. The first mentioned was the lover of Madame Rey, the second, the lover of Madame Montmorency. At some point, the colonels, and presumably the ladies, reached an

agreement to exchange partners, and did so. The two husbands, observing their wives being passed from hand to hand like commodities in the marketplace, were dumbfounded. A great deal of the bitter black coffee was drunk at this time, and I fear that it was the beginning of Montmorency's heart problem. The colonels are on my select list. Today I have been closeted with Marcel, making our arrangements, including choosing the best route to the theatre of war where the curtain is about to go up. I have felt for some time that 'theatre' is the ideal word to describe operations of the Grande Armée. Like most of my thoughts, I keep this to myself. We will need winter clothing, and provisions for ourselves and the horses. Marcel is now insisting that we travel in a berlin. This kind of carriage will provide better protection from the weather than a landau. He also insists that two teams of horses be taken, and two grooms. He estimates that the journey will take ten to fourteen days on the winter roads, but says it is guesswork. The weather forecasts reported in the *Moniteur* are not favourable, therefore, we have no time to waste and will depart at first light tomorrow. I am to dine with Brigadier-General Bertrand this evening and will inform him that I am to be absent on a business trip for several weeks. Of course, I will also tell Therese this. I do not anticipate objections; they are incurious about my movements, about my life in general …

Reading this at 10.30 a.m., the next day, Pierre realised that his conclusion that the mission wouldn't proceed was incorrect. His forebear's enthusiasm for the trip, despite difficulties, was unrelenting – though surely they'd be forced to turn back at some point, probably well before they reached the white-hell surrounding the town of Eylau. Anton and Marcel could not reach Eylau by 8 February! Impossible!

He fetched an atlas and estimated that it was three days' drive on modern roads. But then, the saddle-maker didn't yet know there'd be a battle at Eylau, on 8 February. His plan appeared to be to head for the region where the Grande Armée was massing, taking pot-luck on what battle or battles might eventuate. But the winter roads … And finding Tweedledum and Tweedledee – even if they were engaged in combat, even if they were killed – would be, as he'd noted himself, like hunting for a needle in a haystack.

Make this a thousand haystacks! It would take all the contriving of the Prince of Co-incidence to achieve the saddle-maker's aims, and the prince was Pierre's own exclusive mentor. Or so he thought. His forebear's experience was in leather and business, and in negotiating the nuances of a *ménage à trois*, not in a hare-brained escapade like this.

Pierre shook his head. And, it wasn't an honourable project. But it did offer a new twist for his novel. He told himself: That's immaterial. Anton Brun hadn't featured in his consciousness prior to the discovery of the journal; now Anton's life was entwined with his own. Affection? No doubt at all that he felt this for the saddle-maker. And respect. All in all, the novelist hoped that the proposed latest (ignoble) collection of the man who spoke to him so confidentially and intimately, from the stiff, age-fragrant pages would be abandoned, that he'd come to his senses.

Pierre took up the journal again.

'Chanson', 29 January (continued)

… Yesterday, the preserving bottles and the embalming fluid arrived in boxes that I unpacked myself, and transferred to the cupboards and locked. They wait in readiness. I must confess that I am surprised by the ambition which motivates my new collection. I have recorded the part concerning the orders, medals and insignia, but not that of the other. It is connected to the preserving bottles, and to the sharp-bladed Birmingham knife which I have acquired. I am not a man with friends. Friendship is a talent which has passed me by. In fact, I move in a world of a few acquaintances, business and official – some closer than others, however, such as poor Rey and poor Montmorency. I am an individual who is able to take life's setbacks with a reasonable dose of equanimity, more so than those gentlemen; all that we shared were commonplace conversation, the bitter black coffee – and, the misfortune of our marital circumstances – as we stood like cast-off mannequins in ballroom corners. Yet, I feel a bond with them, and sympathy – also a responsibility to the helpless fellows weighed down, much more than me, under the burden of their betrayal and dishonour. Perhaps, like me, they love their wives. I do not know about this. News has arrived of the passing of Montmorency, so they are both gone … The other: I propose to slice off the appendages of their military tormentors – the organs which have brought both transitory pleasure and indelible pain. Justice and retribution? Some might call it revenge. Who can tell what it is? In the fastness of their great silence, it will mean nothing to those gentlemen. Yet, something to me who is still living and breathing the comedy of life. So the bottles and the fluid await. I imagine the severed members peacefully afloat in their new environment. I am committing these thoughts to my journal, to make the collecting and its purposes that I am to embark upon quite clear in my head …

Pierre lays aside the journal and stands up. As if in a dream, he walks out to the balcony and gazes down at the spreading greenery. He isn't dreaming; he is stunned. For three weeks (it seems much longer), he's been invited into the saddle-maker's life, been steadily coming to terms with his philosophical and dignified character, with the restraint of his suffering, backgrounded by his great love for Therese, and with the apparent growth of ambivalent forgiveness, even warmth, toward his cavalryman cuckolder.

Now, bursting from the narrative, this!

Insanity! He begins to pace the balcony, rubbing his scar. After the first shock, what is he feeling? Disappointment? Really, that had begun with his discovery of the new collection, and the saddle-maker's motives and intentions with it. Now the business to come, with the Birmingham knife, takes it to an evil dimension. Yet, it's one of the turning points that he's been so keen to discover – a basic of his novel. But revenge? Bizarre, barbaric! A thought surfaces, whirls in his brain like a madcap scrap of paper in a fire – a title: *Monsieur Brun's Revenge*. His breath ejaculates in a semi-gasp. He hates it!

Evil dimension? 'Evil' could be interchanged with 'absurd'. Pierre plunges back into the salon, craving black coffee, goes to the kitchen, seizes the pot. Madame Roget, by his side in a flash, takes it from him. 'I will bring it out.'

She gives him her stern, searching look. She has seen this before. Another one of his failed love affairs? Although he's been incommunicado for weeks, she isn't here all the time.

Taking deep breaths, calmer, he returns to the balcony. He realises now how close to the saddle-maker he's become – this forebear who's been gone for two hundred years but whose essence lingers in their apartment, in his brain.

Throughout the days, reading the journal, he's been living in two worlds, and more and more that of the saddle-maker.

Anton, that night on the terrace, when the sabre had flashed in the moonlight, had essayed that the brigadier-general might've taken leave of his senses. Or had the thought been a mask, for the dark current of violent intention running in his own brain?

Madame Roget puts the coffee cup into his hand, has stirred in his one allowed sugar. He sips the steaming brew. It's hot and stronger than usual. On the balcony table, a single white rose is splendid in a thin glass vase. Pierre sees it, recalls the white rose for Anton – two occasions – from Therese. The saddle-maker has been unable to fathom the meaning of these gifts emerging from the twilight surrounding their relations. Pierre wonders if he can. His mind roams further. Perhaps it's not all bad news. He's sure that Bertrand isn't on the list for the Birmingham knife; the stated targets are those who've dishonoured the late Messieurs Rey and Montmorency, and their wives. He considers this. It might be said that in a friendless life, from beyond their graves, his forebear – with strange reasoning and linked to his sense of justice – is consecrating two friendships; thus, not totally ignoble.

Too sentimental, Pierre thinks. So what? He puts the coffee cup beside the rose and goes into the salon. The journal for 1807 is on the table beside his chair. Sunlight streaming through the windows burnishes the leather binding. His place-marker is after the last entry he's read: 29 January. He knows that the next entry is dated 15 March; the longest interval between entries that he's found. Presumably it will be a report on the Prussian journey. At least he survived! He does not wish to read this yet, needs a respite. His eyes do. He will obtain a new prescription for his reading spectacles. He must re-group – again, like Bertrand's light cavalry brigade, like the general with his physical rehabilitation – and renew his working relationship with his unconscious, with the Prince of Imagination, who he senses is becoming restive.

In his mind, he must begin to sort out the structure of his novel. And properly explain his situation to the green-eyed divorcee; he dreamed about her last night, for the first time.

Dear Reader (forgive me this familiarity), I've been present, sitting back in my observer's corner; now I feel impelled to again intervene. Only momentarily. The saddle-maker's story – at least as far as the journal records it – is about to enter its closing phase. 'What?', you might interject. 'Isn't this premature? You've given us no indication that a conclusion is so imminent.' Quite right; however, take my word for it: the closing phase in this affair can be compared to the last act in a three-act play.

In novel-writing, omniscience – in my case, at any rate – is embracing, though not all-embracing. I knew that Pierre was to find out the full dimension of Anton Brun's collecting intentions, but not how he would react. That has been instructional. You may query this as a device. In my role, you either know all, or you know nothing. Isn't that the way it is? Not necessarily. I do know that after he's read the final entry penned by the saddle-maker, on 27 June 1807, he is to step through that 'doorway into a new world' spoken of by his admired John Fowles, and the story will swing into a new direction. Although it could be said, a quite natural direction. He will be excited about this.

He is right to turn to his Prince of Imagination – and thus step beyond the straightjacket of the saddle-maker's story – because it is the only true path for him into the novel, of which he's not yet written a word, not even a note. Nor do I know what he intends to do about the green-eyed lady. (I wish he would give her a name!) I hope it's not to be another mistake in his personal life. Of course, I could know all these things, but not knowing keeps me amused. By the way, he'll need to find a new publisher. The telephone message from his present one, which he's not responded to, was to communicate the termination of their relationship. The sales of his last two books have been 'financially challenged', the phrase deployed in their emails by the publisher's marketing gurus. Their future together has evaporated.

That night in the sledge-bed, dreams chased through Pierre's mind: persons, images, scenes, as if seen through a kaleidoscope. None had any connection with the journal, or his novel, as far as he could recall or determine. His mother was present, serious and pale, sitting in the clinical, white-tiled kitchen, trying to tell him something about the apartment. He had that. But no information came. She bit her lip, her face disappointed. Then he was cold in his prison cell, then awake in Paris in the early hours of an indeed chilly spring morning, with traffic growling in the streets below like the zoo's big cats hungry for breakfast.

Under the warmth of the rose-head shower, his wife said to him, 'Blessed water'. She'd loved it. Tears sprang into his eyes. Five years, and still they came. The saddle-maker's words on friendship were before his eyes. His own friends were few – one from the army, two from university, his wife – all of them passed on, each one an untimely death; of course, a mile of acquaintances. He thought: Is there a genetic hand-me-down from Anton at work in me?

He heard the hall door open: Madame Roget arriving. When he went out for breakfast on the balcony, she said, 'He's failing'.

Pierre stopped and looked at her. 'Shouldn't you be with him?'

'He doesn't wish it. He listens to music all the time, especially Beethoven. He has no pain. They say it will be two, three weeks.'

Nonetheless, she should be with him. But she isn't a person to argue with, even to persuade. The novelist eats his croissant spread with blackberry jam, considers the curt communication, looks at the blue sky, the gentle breeze from the gardens on his face, hearing the cheerful bird-chirping, picturing Monsieur Roget, whom he's never met, lying in his hospice bed with ear-phones on, Beethoven in his ears and brain.

He enters the salon and sits down in his reading chair, but ignores the bulky journal for 1807 on the side-table. The saddle-maker is on his journey to East Prussia – a forlorn hope. Snippets from his past reading, of an unresolved nature, float up in his mind: the Belgian shawl, the special leather prosthesis being crafted in Lille, Therese's white roses, the Birmingham knife. These and a dozen or more other clues, if you like, in Monsieur Brun's narrative, might feature in his novel. The fact is, he won't know the resolution of such matters until he's read Anton's last entry, and then he still mightn't know!

Right now, he's having a sabbatical, re-grouping, including in his personal life. Purposefully, he rises and goes to the telephone in the hall. He looks up numbers and quickly makes three appointments.

During the next three days, he visits his eye specialist and will have new reading spectacles by the weekend, also his dentist for a routine check-up and clean. He thinks about phoning his publisher, but doesn't. He has a good idea what the call is about: mid-list writers are being sent to literary graveyards in a procession of old-fashioned hearses, reflecting the status they've arrived at. He imagines that, and grins at the blue sky. The fellow can talk to his agent, if he can find her. She's a lady who appears to have gone into hibernation.

He catches up with his walking, with a two-hour march around the Jardin du Luxembourg; diabetes in mind. He is not thinking about Anton, or the journal, though each keeps trying to nudge into his consciousness. He's wearing a light-coloured suit, a panama hat, and carrying a bronze-handled cane; the historical novelist, out and about. He grins to himself. If nothing else, he's an actor for his own entertainment.

In the above-mentioned attire, the hat removed, the stick laid aside, he sits at a table outside a bistro in the first *arrondissement*. It's been in business since 1932 and he's been a patron for fifteen years. It's old-fashioned, and has a few luxury dishes on the menu at surprisingly low prices. Pierre can afford the best, but he's frugal with expenditure. The actress was scathing about that, but he's not waiting for her.

Here she comes, swinging down the short street in her long-legged stride, a small green hat on the side of her head, burnished leather bag – he's an eye for leather now – slung over her shoulder. The green eyes have found him. His heart jumps a little. He hasn't plotted this meeting out: a few apologies, a minimal explanation of his preoccupation, then a friendly silence? Let her talk. He's in observer mode, wishes to assess this woman's character (or try to), to judge where she is coming from (or attempt to). He stands up; they shake hands, and exchange a formal kiss.

'So good of you to come, Lucile', he says.

'So good of you to ask me, Pierre.' She smiles. There's no intonation of 'at last' in her voice, or manner.

They talk about the circumstances of their first meeting – at an exhibition of paintings by an artist they both know. No one introduced them; side-by-side, looking at a volcano-like whorl of red paint, they'd struck up a conversation. She loved a volcano, she said, its flaming force; he was less keen. The exhibition hadn't sold so well, she informed him today. The waiter, a grizzled veteran known to Pierre as Jules, brought the menu and suggested the cold lobster with their special mayonnaise. He remembered that Pierre almost always ordered it. They conferred and agreed: lobster. Pierre mentions a wine, and she nods her dark head.

They regard each other. Next step, down to business, thinks Pierre. He explains the situation he's working under, the germination of the new novel – up to a point. She listens attentively, doesn't make comments, and for once, for the moment, he is happy to talk – hasn't been doing much of that lately, except in his head. She was vivacious when he'd seen her in the party on Sunday, at the Jardin du Luxembourg. Today, a more sedate, thoughtful person looks into his eyes.

Pierre is deciding about this woman – although perhaps he has already, otherwise why is he here? – about the calm, restrained persona now impressing itself on his mind. But everyone has their different faces, he warns himself.

'Can you wait a little longer?' He is in earnest. 'Until I'm well-set in the writing routine. See the way ahead more clearly.' God, he's skating on thin ice. The forthright main-chancer! Why hadn't he just said: I'd like to make love to you, but ...

She can wait. He leans back. They enjoy the lobster, and the Sancerre, and the fruit tart that follows. In a pleasant, relaxed mode, they discuss their few mutual acquaintances. She doesn't linger, departs for an appointment, they don't kiss again; briefly, she touches the back of his hand, leaves him to sit in the sunshine finishing the Sancerre, drinking a cup of coffee.

He watches her go in the direction of the Louvre, her tall, swinging figure, the green hat disappear into the street crowd. He is thinking about friendship. The kind he had with his wife. It seems a possibility with this green-eyed woman named Lucile, as it hadn't been with the actress, or the red-haired investment banker, or the one or two others; there'd been a kind of competitive, hard-edged aspect to those liaisons, a repetitive pattern that he must break out of.

At their first meetings, the actress and the investment banker had asked him about his scar; she hadn't and it seemed a good omen.

He shakes Jules's hand and leaves. Back to his other business. Two questions have winged into his mind: Have both the saddle-maker and the cavalryman, from their different causes, gone insane? Is Therese's illness moving toward a tragic conclusion?

He will collect his new spectacles, re-open the 1807 journal this evening, and recommence the search for these and other answers.

'Chanson', 15 March 1807

I have re-entered the land of the living. For the past week, I have been confined to bed – with a chill in my lungs, my surgeon says. Breathing has certainly been difficult and quite painful. Thankfully, I am a resilient fellow and with a return to warmth, glasses of hot milk, and my cook's chicken broth, I am today up and about. Sadly, one of the grooms who accompanied me on the misconceived journey has expired. It is my duty to make arrangements for his family. They will have a cottage and a pension. Marcel, I believe, blames himself for the failings of the mission; however, the responsibility lies with me alone, and today I will tell him so. At this point, I do not wish to dwell on the horrors, and discomforts, that we encountered. I wish to give these matters a period of sober reflection. I will record a brief outline of our experience, as already much of it is a blur in my mind, and I fear details will slip from my memory – although it might be best if they do. The respective condition of the roads, weather, and the poverty-stricken nature of the terrain we traversed, combined to make the attainment of our destination impossible. East Prussia might as well have been on the moon. We did not cover even half the distance. Certainly, it has showed me what a naive fellow I am in respect of geography, and distance. The journey to the border of our country was far from smooth, but uneventful compared to what was to come. We lost a wheel about fifty kilometres from the frontier, but Marcel was able to put matters right. The weather deteriorated on passing into Prussia, as did the roads. A miserable succession of flea-infested, freezing inns, with bad food and surly service – even when such were available – followed. Most days, we did not travel twenty kilometres. It was impossible to obtain reliable information of the way ahead, and the occasional passing couriers, going to and from Paris, were unhelpful. No doubt the frozen fellows wondered why we were there. The other few encounters with our own military on the road were unpleasant. One such stands out. In the middle of nowhere, a sergeant of dragoons with two troopers demanded that we surrender our spare team. I had taken the precaution of obtaining a letter, signed and sealed, from the Ministry, as a passport against such requisitions which I know are a speciality of the Grande Armée, but in the way the sergeant inspected it, I doubted if he understood its significance. I waved my arms around in an endeavour to press this home. However, I am sure that it was the unwavering aim of Marcel's pistols levelled at his breast that persuaded the sergeant to wheel away, and depart. The following day, in the midst of a brutal snowstorm, I shouted to Marcel: 'Enough!' We turned around and headed for home. I must admit, it seemed another impossible destination. The other groom, despite my precautions with fur-clothing, scarves and hats, is suffering from frost-bite to the nose, and my surgeon says that it is problematical whether he will keep it.

As he reads the entry, Pierre, new spectacles on his nose, feels that he is back at the coalface of his impending novel, which throughout his brief sabbatical has been in waiting, like a soup simmering on the hob. He pauses as if to regain breath, gazes out the salon windows at the sky. The last entry validates his previous conclusion on the fate of the expedition. He's pleased to note the saddle-maker's admission of his naivety – a human touch, befitting his forebear. Hopefully, it might influence him to abandon this new collection and its grotesque, inhuman character.

He reads on:

'Chanson', 15 March 1807 (continued)
… Therese has been most solicitous during my recovery from the rigours just mentioned. She came to my door with a bowl of warm stewed fruits with ginger. She is so thin and delicate, and my concern for her is increasing. She gave me the palest of smiles as she enquired about my health. The surgeon is reticent, and says only that her diet requires more nourishing food, and she must avoid chills at all costs. I was pleased to see her gown was of warm material, up to the neck, with the Belgian shawl over her shoulders, I suppose for decoration. She was a vision, and I was entranced. I have asked the cook about her diet; the woman is of sound country stock and knows about wholesome

foods and herbal remedies. I fear the problem will be to entice my dear wife to take a sufficient quantity. This morning, I passed my son in the corridor on his way to the school room with his tutor. He stopped and bowed to me. I patted his head. He appears to be a shy little fellow. Last evening, Brigadier-General Bertrand came to my apartment, bringing one of my fine cognacs. I was helped from bed by my servant, wrapped in rugs, and sat with the cavalryman before the fire. The first sip of the liquor made me cough violently. He may be curious at my long absence, and the condition of our party on return; nevertheless, as is his way, he asked no questions. He is stronger and has resumed his morning rides. He is experimenting with the leather attachment to his left arm. I was delighted to learn that it is giving him reasonable management of the reins. We never discuss Therese, although I would like to question him on his idea of her health. I think he is brooding on the Emperor's future intentions in Prussia, and with the Russians – and, on the terrible battle at Eylau. He did mention that his brigade was not involved in that slaughter. When taking his leave, he gripped my hand, and I was quite moved. There seemed to be a strong emotion in the gesture. I sense that he is planning a return to duty. Many papers wait on my desk, and I am anxious to take up the reins of my business ... Lying abed during my recovery, I have considered the new collection. Collecting has always been in my blood, and my butterfly and clock collections are the dearest to my heart; I now regard them as complete. What is their fate? I ponder this. I wonder if my young son will inherit my passion, or whether they will, when my life is finis, be dispersed with all the lovely things in 'Chanson' … I will be brief and plain. I have decided to abandon the new collection. The aborted attempt to reach East Prussia was instructional, but it is not the main reason for my decision. It is sufficient to say that I believe its conception was an aberration of my character. I see the whole situation, which prompted my rash intentions, in a clearer light. I am a meek man, and pleased to be so; the dish of revenge has never been on my menu, and I know now never will be.

Pierre puts the volume aside, and removes his spectacles with a flourish. A tide of quiet exultation moves in him. 'Bravo, Anton', he murmurs, looking down the room to where the large oriental vase shimmers in the morning sun. His forebear's humane character stands redeemed. It calls for a celebration. He goes to the kitchen, takes a bottle of Vouvray from the refrigerator and uncorks it.

Madame Roget, stirring a fish soup at the stove observes his buoyant mood. 'Lunch will be ready in ten minutes.'

'Wonderful!', he says, and pauses. 'Monsieur?'

'Unchanged. Yesterday he listened to Beethoven. The Fourth Symphony.' Dourly, she stirred. Pierre imagines that she's never listened herself to that least celebrated of the composer's symphonies. Nor to any of them. He is sure that she is a dutiful wife, but probably there are pools of silence, of non-sharing, in their married life. She never plays music while she works, though perhaps that's in consideration of his quiet time.

Sunlight filters through the trees, frets cheerfully on the balcony table, as he eats the soup and the home-made bread. Therese remains a shadow in his head – a wraith-like vision, just as the saddle-maker recorded. He wonders if a portrait of her has survived; surely Anton would have had one painted. He muses on the possibility, and sips Vouvray – an ideal if fortuitous matching with the fish soup. He imagines the painting hanging in a country house: a portrait of an unknown lady, circa 1800, unsigned by the artist. He will do a search on the internet, but is unconfident of success. Doubtless, many hundreds of such portraits exist in France, now rendered anonymous by the break-up of estates, the passage of time; the pale, transparent skin of their faces and their revealed bosoms, pointing as well as anything else to the transient nature of our existence, of eras. His earlier fear about her health is heightened.

However, his apprehension concerning the sanity of the two men in her life has receded. The violent swish of Bertrand's sabre that night on the terrace, which nearly decapitated the saddle-maker, could be put down to an outbreak of frustration or other natural emotion. And Anton is back on course, back in his calm and humane persona.

Pierre enjoys the hot soup, and thinks of the groom's frost-bitten nose.

After supper that evening, Pierre settled in for a long session. He is determined to finish the last volume tonight. The tide was quickening, not so much in the events that the saddle-maker was committing to the thick, rough-edged paper with his ink-splattering pen, but in the various undercurrents that the novelist sensed beneath the surface of the lives he was so avidly studying. Beneath the surface of the lives of his characters, that was the nub. Anton Brun was very clear and very close to him; the brigadier-general had a firm foothold in his mind, though there was work to do.

Therese was the problem. She remained as elusive as morning mist. There must be letters from her, which would open up her personality. Had any survived? He'd had this thought the other day. With her, much more than the others, he'll need to call on the Prince of Imagination – if that figment in his mind is patient enough to stick around.

In the recovery period following the Prussian ordeal, the saddle-maker dropped back into the embrace of his beloved 'Chanson'. Day after day, he sat in the nooks and crannies of the château, gazing at the splendid rooms, or from the windows at vistas of his park, where the trees were now filigreed with new leaves. All of it was balm to his mind and body. At certain points in the recent expedition, he'd feared that he would never see it again.

In the evenings, he remained in his study, dealing with business correspondence. His factories were working at full capacity. The Grande Armée was re-fitting, reorganising and, in particular, re-mounting many of its cavalry regiments. The Emperor's prestige after the butchery of Eylau had suffered a severe blow. However, he'd ordered a third levy of conscripts in a year and assembled 300,000 men. 'The game is afoot, once more', the saddle-maker recorded in the brownish, sloping script. The novelist smiled: One of his own phrases.

Pierre read on, into the spring and early summer months. Therese's health improved with the warmer weather. Bravo! Anton wrote that Bertrand continued to take tea each afternoon in her apartment. Pierre speculated on whether this was the only form of intercourse in which they now engaged. It seemed likely in view of the state of her health. On 4 April, Anton wrote:

The general is now spending most of each morning on horse-back, practising his management of the reins. I am delighted to see how much control he now has with my device. He expresses himself as being well pleased with it. Yesterday, I sat on the terrace for an hour watching him. After various manoeuvres, he finished with a charge across the park at full gallop, sabre extended, followed by my grooms whooping in their excitement. I'm pleased to say that, to my people, he is much the celebrity in residence.

Otherwise, life in the household, on the estate, moved in a sedate, pastoral rhythm, in concord with his forebear's quiet thoughts.

After midnight, Pierre left his illuminated corner in the salon and went to the kitchen to make coffee. Waiting for it to brew, the idea that had been hovering over him for several days (much like the mist that he'd ascribed to Therese's character, even her existence) materialised in his mind like a gleaming, new-minted coin: At the end of the saddle-maker's journal and its story, whatever its conclusion, he must step through John Fowles' doorway, into a new world; for the imaginative development of his novel, he must do this. The Prince of Imagination is already scouting the terrain ahead (not to say that Pierre won't have a creative role in filling in gaps in the saddle-maker's history); but in essence, Anton Brun's narrative of the *ménage à trois* will be the foundation – for another story.

'I'm looking for a continuum into 2012', he tells himself, though he doesn't yet know how he will do it, or what it will involve. Carrying a cup and the coffee pot, he pauses in the hall, listening. The gardens below luxuriate in a humid silence. Yet, behind him in the big apartment, there are faint rustlings. He tilts his head. Anton's here tonight. Perhaps examining the books in his library – the religious ones? The novelist believes that he'll soon need the consolation of religion.

It's nearly 1 a.m. when Pierre moves into the circle of light over his chair.

'Chanson', 10 April 1807
This morning, Therese's personal maid brought a
tissue-wrapped parcel to my rooms. My dear wife has
had six silk white shirts made for me in Paris. It is the
only such gift she has ever given me. I am delighted –
and astonished. I went to the window to contemplate
this event. The sky is without cloud, and the birds
are singing in the park. In a certain way, that I do
not understand, I am in her thoughts. I walked to my
study. In the front hall, I heard the clatter of boots and
the jingle of spurs. The brigadier-general was going
for his ride. Several days ago, a letter was delivered to
him from the Ministry. He read it immediately in the
hall and then walked out to the terrace. Motionless,
at the far balustrade, he gazed out across the park for
quite some time. That night we dined together, and he
told me that the colonels of his regiments would be
arriving on the next Tuesday morning. I offered him
a private luncheon with them, which he accepted.
They arrived in a berlin very much like the one I took
to Prussia. To myself, I called them 'the three hawks'.
Their lean, weathered faces and spare bodies made
that impression on me. Although remarkably similar
in appearance, they are of course not the three who

came here before. Lamentably, they are dead. Last night, we dined together again. He did not refer to the visit, but the *Moniteur* is cautiously reviewing the political situation with Russia. I fear that he will be leaving us soon, but yesterday evening, over the cognac, he wished to talk only of 'Chanson'. He has read my book with great attention, and asked several questions in his terse way. I conjecture that a feeling has grown in him for the château, which is akin to my own. More and more I perceive that he is a man of sensibility, beyond what one would expect – taking into account the nature of his profession and his experience. I have thought this for some time. He has spent his life in military quarters and barracks, and has never had a quiet haven to himself. He has found one at 'Chanson'. I am gratified. The other day, turning a corner in my corridors, I saw him talking to my young son in a kindly manner. He patted the boy on the head. The lad spoke with a vivacity I had not seen before. I withdrew, unseen.

Pierre's vision was blurring. It was after 2 a.m. and the coffee was cold. He set the last volume aside, removed his spectacles and rubbed his eyes. Not far to go now, but he wouldn't reach the end tonight. The sledge-bed waited. A thought came: The rich patina of its oak bed-head might be burnished with the dreams of his forebear – and his own. Fanciful. The Prince of Imagination would strike it out with his blue pencil. Trial and error; everything about his trade was.

Pierre was woken by the telephone. It was Madame Roget. Monsieur had passed away during the night. He listened, and spoke his condolences. She sounded as usual, except for a slight catch in her voice. She would be absent for a week. Could she make temporary arrangements for him? He reassured her that it would be unnecessary. Sitting on the edge of the bed, he wondered if Monsieur had died with his ear-phones on. She mentioned two made-up dishes in the freezer. From experience, he knew that such prosaic considerations could distract one from grief.

Pierre showered, and under the flow of warm water waited for illuminations on the way ahead; none came this morning. Nor had he any dreams that he could recall, to fall back on. He went down to the street and around the corner to the *pâtisserie* for croissants. He bought only one. Back in his kitchen, he heated coffee. Walking by the gardens, his thoughts had been on Anton and his puzzling relations with his long-term guest. It was obvious that the saddle-maker's ambivalence towards the cavalryman had been shifting in its balance to – one might even say – an affectionate position. Was his forebear fully conscious of the change? From some recent entries, an inference could be taken that he was. It was remarkable in the circumstances, but each was a remarkable man in his own way, and the circumstances had gone far beyond the norm. Pierre wondered where it would end.

Today, or tonight, he would finish the journal.

'Chanson', 15 April 1807
This morning, I read of an event in the *Moniteur*, which both shocked and astonished me. I have hardly recovered from it yet. And I fear it will greatly trouble

me into the future. After breakfast each morning, for the past week, the general and I have taken to reading the newspapers in a sunlit corner of the library. We don't often converse; nonetheless, I find it a companionable experience breaking the solitary habit of my adult life. The news we read is often disturbing, but what I read at 9 a.m. today was so momentous to me that I herewith transcribe the article into my journal: 'Monday. Shocking Murders in Paris. On Sunday evening, at approximately 8 p.m., in a house of entertainment on Rue de Rivoli, Colonel Hubert Moreau and Colonel Michel Tallien, respectively commanding officers of the 17th and 19th Light Infantry regiments, were shot and killed by another guest of the establishment. It is alleged by the police that the assassin was identified as Rupert Montmorency, aged 21, who made good his escape from the infamous scene. The alleged assassin is the eldest son of the late industrialist Monsieur Montmorency and Madame Montmorency. The deputy head of the police advises that immediately following the murders, a bestial and savage act was perpetrated on the corpses of the two unfortunate officers. The police have begun a widespread search.' The printed words struck me like a thunderbolt: Colonels Tweedledum and Tweedledee! Deliberately, I put the paper aside. The article was on the *Moniteur*'s front page. Brigadier-General Bertrand reached across and took up the paper. In my shocked state, I watched him as if mesmerised. He must be reading it, must at least know of the victims. 'Humph', he grunted after a few moments and turned the page. I hurriedly excused myself and left the room. In an agitated state, I paced the terrace. The poor young man.

I knew him only slightly, but I recalled a conversation with his father one night in one of those hateful ballrooms, shortly after the colonels, in their profligate way, had passed Madame Montmorency from one to the other. Monsieur Montmorency obliquely glanced at me as Madame glided past in the arms of Tweedledee, said, 'My son Rupert is very much disturbed by this latest business. He is a hot-headed young fellow. He abhors military men.' He shook his head, as if a kind of slow fuse to a mine was sizzling in their family's future. How accurate his premonition! When the father died, I should have been alert and stepped in to offer counsel to the young fellow. He was left alone to navigate the sea of dishonour and hate that he doubtless saw himself afloat upon. I admit that I emitted a groan. I saw now, even more clearly, how misconceived my proposed plan for new collecting had been. Pursuit of justice and acts of posthumous friendship had been my intention, but a far worthier course would have been to intervene in the situation and to dissuade the young fellow from his vengeful notions. I continued to pace back and forth, thinking how I had failed the family, my own intention of friendship. In the roughest of ways, justice had been done. The law, however, does not take that view. They will chop off his head if they catch him. The only hope is for him to escape abroad. If he is brought to trial, I will place all my resources at his disposal. I became aware that Therese's maid, followed by the general, had hurried onto the terrace. The stiff-starched woman's face was as white as her pristine bodice. 'Monsieur! Madame is coughing up blood! I have sent post-haste for the surgeon.' Another, the cruellest dagger, into my heart!

Pierre stands up and stretches, as much in reaction to this dramatic information as to ease his back. The tips of his fingers find the scar. Food for thought here, he thinks, looking down at the journal page for 15 April; and in his scar, though he keeps that on the back-burner. Remembering, he glances at his watch. Noon. He has a funeral to dress for, and go to. He has time to eat. Earlier, he'd taken one of Madame Roget's made-up dishes from the freezer. He goes to the kitchen and puts it in the microwave. When it's done, he carries the plate and a glass of white wine out to the balcony. *Quiche lorraine*, one of her more delicate concoctions. 'God bless you', he murmurs.

And you, Anton, he thinks. The writing's on the wall for Therese. And for young Montmorency. In the latter case, he's sure that the guilt the saddle-maker is feeling will soften as he comes back onto his usual pragmatic course. In the final analysis, his forebear is a survivor, and he admires that. Affairs are affairs, but those colonels, with their cynical *modus operandi* in that field, had it coming; whatever the Code Napoleon said about it (if anything), or the moral mores of the day (not that much, he imagines), they really did. They should pass the colonels' medals to young Montmorency!

It was a resolution that Pierre liked, for his fictional purposes, though the young fellow's calling in the deadly duellist from Lyons would've been even better; the round, red faces of Tweedledum and Tweedledee would've made great targets for the merciless apple-shooting merchant. He could be the champion of the meek, cuckolded non-duellers! Pierre thought: Nothing to stop me bending history a bit.

He dresses in a dark suit and puts on a black tie. His father wore black ties to funerals and Pierre does, too. Not their style to wear a bright, celebration-of-life one. In their opinion, a tie at a funeral should match the sombre tolling of the church bell.

More people were at the cemetery than he'd expected. The sun appeared in fits and starts as the priest read the service, and spoke a brief eulogy. Madame Roget stood amid a conclave of black-garbed friends and relatives, mainly women. The Rogets had no children, he knew. On arrival, he'd shaken her hand and given his condolences again, and now he retreated to the background. The cemetery was small, no more than a hectare, and quite steep. His eyes moved over the conglomeration of marble statuary, and up the hill to the high brick boundary wall; conclaves of grounded, white marble angels overwhelmed the human figures present.

His thoughts drifted beyond the priest's monotone. His forebear, it seemed, would soon be facing up to a similar scene. He imagined that he'd conduct himself with all the dignity of Madame Roget … 'A bestial and savage act.' Was it possible that young Montmorency had, unknowingly, taken a leaf out of the saddle-maker's book? At least, the one he'd planned to write then abandoned.

As soon as the service ends, he'll return to the journal. '*Quiche lorraine*?', Madame Roget murmurs as he stands before her in farewell, and he nods.

Pierre did not return immediately to his apartment; instead he walked thirty minutes across to the Right Bank, and reached the Place des Vosges. He found the building and looked up at the windows of the third floor. Behind some of those windows was Lucile's apartment. On a whim, he'd wished to fix the geography in his mind – where the green-eyed woman, who seemed to float in his future like a serene promise, hung her green hat. He must hurry up with his project. White roses were on Monsieur Roget's coffin, and now Therese's gifts, brought to the saddle-maker in his apartment at 'Chanson', glowed in his mind.

Not on a whim – he'd been planning this – he retraced his steps and then detoured to an auction house in a street not far from Monsieur Jacques' restaurant.

The cutting weapons were in a large glass case mounted on one wall. Swords from every Continental army of the 1700s and 1800s were ranged there – some, ornate examples in seemingly mint condition; others, tarnished specimens, undecorated, bearing the marks of hard usage, possibly deadly usage. He'd examined a colour picture on the internet of the hussar ordinary-issue sabre in service in the early 1800s, and he'd wanted to take it further.

The one that the attendant took out for him was a dull but formidable blade, slightly serrated in one portion of its edge – a curved blade made for hacking and slicing, not thrusting. 'This is not an officer's weapon', the man said. Pierre thought: I wouldn't be so definitive about that. The man continued: 'Remarkably, it has a provenance. It came to us from a family in Liège whose ancestor served as a trooper with the 3rd Brigade of Hussars at the Battle of Friedland in 1807.' Pierre held it. It had a lovely balance in his hand. He didn't ask the price, wouldn't buy it. This was enough.

He left the shop. A strong, cool breeze presaging rain assailed his face. He relished the sensation; he was heading back into 1807.

'Chanson', 16 April 1807

Therese is resting comfortably this morning. I am told that two medical men will be here from Paris in the early afternoon. My surgeon stayed with her until late yesterday. I suspect that it was not the first bleeding she has suffered. Her personal servants are evasive about this, and I will not press the point. She may well have instructed them to remain silent. If it is so, I can only guess at her motive. Whatever the answer, the future course and treatment is the question of prime importance. My surgeon wishes to consult with his colleagues before discussing the situation. I fear I know what the disease is; every family of our generation has had its cases ... Today the general, almost ceaselessly, is again patrolling the corridors as he did when recovering from the loss of his arm. It is exhausting to observe him, and I am concerned for his well-being. I will try to entice him to dine with me this evening ... I have only just been able to look at the *Moniteur*. There is no additional news on the murders – executions, I prefer to call them – or on young Montmorency's whereabouts. A packet of letters has arrived from my factory; I do not have the heart to look at them today. I have been thinking of the children – what this may mean. As usual, they are being cared for by the servants who, I believe, take pains with them as if they were their own.

Before rising from his chair, Pierre checked the date of the next entry: 1 May. He read the opening sentence, mournfully shook his head, removed his spectacles, and rubbed his eyes. Spring showers had swept his precinct during the late afternoon, and the light was fading early. From the salon window, he stared down at the murky scene of dripping trees and plants; electric lights now bloomed along the garden's paths. He pictured the cemetery where he'd been earlier in the afternoon: wet, gloomy and deserted. But not lonely for the souls there. Without irony, or humour, he thought: Maybe, at this moment, Monsieur Roget is being introduced into the community by a welcoming committee.

The white roses would be bedraggled, though Madame Roget might have taken them home – she's a thrifty person.

Pierre walked to the kitchen and poured a glass of red wine. Not Chambertin tonight, but a rough young Bordeaux that he used, with its wallop to the palate, to haul himself back to the grindstone. Snippets of his recent reading shuffled in his mind. Bertrand, when he'd read of the murders, had turned the page without comment. The novelist imagined that the kind of event depicted would be, if not par for the course, at least not new to the cavalryman. The fellow's own past wasn't lily-white; possibly there were husbands in his background not as meek, or as calm in temperament, or one could say as humane as the saddle-maker.

On another tack, it appeared Anton was intimating that Therese might've been concealing her illness to protect him; this, like her gifts to him of the white roses, the shirts, were obviously giving the saddle-maker pause for thought.

But I'm thinking in clichés, Pierre told himself.

He resolved to find a Belgian shawl. The sabre was now a clear image to him. The near impossibility of a portrait's surviving (if one had ever existed), with her wearing the beloved gift, teased his mind. He'd found no clues on the internet. When he sat down, however, to write his version of the story, it wouldn't be an insoluble problem for the Prince of Imagination.

'Chanson', 1 May 1807
'Monsieur Brun, I very much regret to inform you that there can be only one outcome to Madame's illness.' These were the words of my surgeon after the conference with his colleagues, two weeks past. She must rest and follow the diet that they have prescribed. If she is assiduous in this, she will have longer. I feel the despair which every loving and dutiful husband must have when confronted with such news. She has ever been a bright but frail spirit. There is a throbbing pain in my heart, as I contemplate an end to it. I cannot find the words to convey my feelings … I have decided to devote less time to my journal. In the scheme of our lives, it no longer seems important. There is one ray of sunlight, however. For the past week, I have been invited each afternoon to join Therese and Bertrand for tea in her apartment. One looks for scraps of happiness in our circumstances, and for me this is most certainly one of them. It is, I believe, another gift to me. She lies in her bed, wearing the Belgian shawl and smiles in turn at each of us. Sometimes the children are brought in for a few moments and kiss their mother. The general says little – of course, he is incapable of normal conversation – so I am left to find a few interesting topics to discourse upon. I comment on the children's growth and health; on matters concerning the estate and our farms; on any important news from Paris; on the seasonal forecast. The half-hour passes quickly and then I leave them. Afterwards, I cannot recall tasting

the tea … Yesterday, I received a letter from Madame Montmorency. A letter distraught and tear-stained; she despairs for her son. She has no news of him. She implores my advice. I must respond promptly, but what to say is troubling me. His only chance, as I have written before, it to find a haven abroad. Her family and friends should not attempt to locate him – if he is still in France, or on the Continent – for the police would be hot on their heels. Her family is trapped in the wreckage of her prodigal life. Nothing may, of course, be said of this; so many families are in similar, if less dramatic, straits. She did not refer to the colonels … The general is spending even more time each day with his horses. The Emperor has unfinished business with Russia; that will be the next cloud on our horizon. The rough with the smooth, I fear.

'Friedland', Pierre breathed. The battle had been fought on 14 June – only six weeks in the future of the inhabitants of 'Chanson' – and Brigadier-General Bertrand was fit for active duty. He'd consult his reference books on the forthcoming battle.

He fried eggs and bacon for his supper. The rough red was very satisfactory with the dish. There were only about twenty pages left to complete his marathon read. Yet again he'd been tempted to plunge on to the end, but yet again he'd held himself back. A wine should be drunk in leisurely, thoughtful sips, and modest mouthfuls; savoured, extracting the full essence, and the journal was the same. Also, he believed that it was the pace his mind, and his unconscious, could best cope with.

The journal finished in 1807; Anton's life had continued

until 1820 – at 'Chanson', and here in this apartment. He mused on those facts. Mysterious terrain lay beyond the journal; he didn't need to know of it. He was exhausted, yet exhilarated, and he took both conditions to the sledge-bed.

At 8.20 the next morning, he thought: The narrative in the journal is the base for my novel – the base only. Half an hour ago, under the even fall of water from the rose-head shower, the way ahead for him flashed into his mind: a clear blueprint. Not the detail that would float up in thousands of particulars from his unconscious, as he sat down each morning to write, including the turning points, as certain in fiction as in life, but the broad scenario. From past experience, he was confident that this was the way it would go. Unless his mind decided to give up the ghost!

'Chanson', 10 May 1807

Today the château has been bathing in sunshine and fine breezes. The sky is a pristine blue. The doors and windows stood open. I lingered outside Therese's apartment on my way to breakfast. I was amazed to hear her singing. My dear brave wife! Tears came into my eyes, the dullness in my heart lifted. A sense of happiness came into it. Admittedly, it was bitter-sweet; nevertheless, I went on with a lighter step. I must strengthen myself for the journey we are on. I have noticed that my shoulders have set into a slump. I must bear up. I am not yet a widower, and, even then … Tonight I dined with Brigadier-General Bertrand. He eats sparsely, and I have instructed the servants to give him modest servings on the plate, so that he may be encouraged to at least eat that amount. Yesterday, fresh samples from the factory arrived for my approval.

My apartment is suffused with their heady aroma. Leather is meat and drink to me, and will be until the day I die. Bertrand talked of cavalry subjects, giving opinions in terse statements almost as if dictating edicts for a training manual. He criticises the French cavalry in its care of horses. Other Continental armies are far superior in their husbandry. To the French horseman, his mount is expendable. He will carelessly turn it into a cornfield at night to graze, the next morning, just as carelessly, shoot the bloated animal for the cookhouse. 'But not in my regiments', he grunted. 'The men would be shot also.' I wonder if this is true. His own mounts are of Arab stock. He says that they are not as fast as European warm-bloods, but more sure-footed, and of superior endurance. The Emperor has purchased thousands of the French horse Boulonnais of Flanders for his *cuirassiers*. He also purchases many Holsteiners for the heavy cavalry. I am aware of some of this related to saddle orders from the Ministry. Bertrand had dressed in one of his fine uniforms, and once again its gilded appointments glittered in the candle-light. We drank the Emperor's health, as usual, in Chambertin. I relish this wine. It is both generous and bright in the mouth.

It was after nine when Pierre left the apartment to walk around the corner to the *pâtisserie*. Yesterday's rain had sluiced down the city, and polished the myriad leaves in the Jardin des Plantes to an even greener lustre. A panoramic blue sky arced over the metropolis, expectant of nothing but good. Walking briskly, he imagined it as a duplicate of the one that the saddle-maker had memorialised above 'Chanson' on 10 May 1807.

He brought home a croissant, and a crusty loaf of bread.

On the balcony, he drank his coffee, and ate the croissant with blackberry jam.

Looking down to the gardens, he recalled Lucile's standing there gazing up at him, and that recent day when, in turn, he'd gazed up at her windows from the Place des Vosges. Already, in his mind, there seemed to be a fine silken thread connecting them. Would it be strong enough to last? Did he wish it to? He grimaced. Novelistic conjecture …

'Chanson', 10 May (continued)

… After dinner, we walked back and forth on the
terrace. The evening air was soft and warm. Birds
were still chirping but quietly, in anticipation of rest. I
believe that we will have a fine, hot summer. Bertrand
put his right arm through my left and we paced
together, arm-in-arm. I have never walked like this with
another human being, man or woman. It was a strange
experience; one that warmed my heart. A week ago,
my lawyer came to 'Chanson'. The general wished to
re-write his will, and he has done so, and entrusted it
to my care. He said: 'Your son. There is a trunk in my
rooms which contains my library of volumes on cavalry
subjects. I wish him to have them. My other assets, my
pension, I have left to my daughter – as you will see – in
trust, as that lawyer fellow calls it.' We were silent for a
while, until he said: 'I have been called back. Tomorrow,
I leave to join my brigade. Tonight, I informed Therese.'
I could only listen. A sense of inevitability rose in me.
The three of us are set in the final stage of our journey

– toward our destiny? Overwhelmingly, I feel this. I cannot find words to state it in the way that I wish to. And, I feel that it is best that I do not try. Certain things in my life are becoming too hard for me. I say only that my heart is the heavier for this news.

Pierre let the journal fall onto his lap. Poor Anton! The gathering shadows in his life were infiltrating his mind, his bloodstream. Thank God, he'd written this narrative; otherwise he'd never have known his forebear, never have established the strong intimacy with the extraordinary – to him, anyway – saddle-maker. His life and times would have remained unknown to his descendant.

Forget his novel! It was inconsequential, compared to all the foregoing.

On a sudden impulse, he left his reading chair and the salon, and crossed the hall to the library. He turned on lights and his eyes searched the high shelves. Here! The brigadier-general's books, in their original bindings, shelved up high, in a corner – about fifty of them. Even so, it was a wonder that at some point in his life he hadn't noticed them. In his young, curious days, however, this room had had little attraction for him. 'Dust', his mother had said. 'Cash', the red-haired investment banker had hissed, nudging him. Respectively, abiding passions for each.

During the morning, Pierre read up on the Battle of Friedland. There was a lot on the internet, including retrospective paintings of the battle scenes. One historian claimed the battle as the zenith of the Emperor's fortunes.

The investment banker was one of those who'd asked him about his scar. 'Did it happen in your army service?' How he wished that were the case. His scars from that time were invisible: a damaged sciatic nerve from heavy landings. He gazed toward the salon's windows. He realised, suddenly, that the saddle-maker's narrative, absorbing him these past weeks, had pushed back the depression that'd stalked him like a hyena during the past five years. He thought: That's nearly been the end of me.

He'd finish the journal today. It was time. Consciously, he'd been primed to push ahead and learn all there was to know in the volumes. Unconsciously, he felt that he'd had the brakes on – as if apprehensive of a deeply negative climax. He'd become too entwined in the saddle-maker's fate. Beside this, the novel that he hoped to write was a tentative shadow, blueprint and all. But today, he'd bite the bullet. With irritated amusement, he muttered: 'Yet again, thinking in clichés'.

'Chanson', 11 May 1807

When I awoke before dawn, last night's interlude on the terrace returned to me. On this dreaded day, Therese, already, will be awake. I listened for the birds, and as I did so, the first chirpings came. But there were other sounds. I rose from my bed and went to the window, guessing what I would see. I looked down, beyond the terrace, to the gravelled area leading to the drive. About seventy horses, their breath steaming in the air, were drawn up in an extended line, a cavalryman standing at the head of each. The men were as still as statues, as if not to disturb the household; the horses, shaking their harness, were making the sounds I had heard. I dressed hurriedly. When I went out to the corridor, I perceived that my household was very much awake. Downstairs in the hall, two officers, their hussar shakos held under their arms, sprang to attention when I appeared. My servants were bringing down the brigadier-general's campaign chest. I walked out to the terrace. The morning was cool and the light came flowing across the park from the east. At the end of the terrace, a crowd from the estate had assembled. Obviously, news of the general's imminent departure had spread overnight. When I re-entered the house, a little procession – the servants carrying Therese, seated on a chair – was coming along a corridor to the hall. They placed her near the front door and tucked a rug around her frail body. This morning, another gift for me: a wan smile and a little nod, as if in acknowledgement that she, and I, were partners in this painful occasion. Brigadier-General Bertrand arrived without ceremony and the officers, hurriedly donning their shakos, again sprang to attention and saluted. Then they clattered and jingled out the door. I felt that I was taking in every detail with a distinct clarity – in anticipation of making this record. Bertrand is well practised at departures. There is no lingering. I am aware that he went to Therese's apartment last night after our time on the terrace. I am sure that he would have said, in his brief way, all he wished to say. He stood before her chair, took her hand in his, and kissed it. He paused where I stood, and shook my hand. I do not think he looked at my face, and I could not look at his. I have asked myself if we were both thinking at this moment: Is this the end? A command was given as he went out; the troop mounted, and the officers saluted again. As they did each morning, my grooms assisted him into the saddle of his Arab mount. It was now light. I noted that my device was affixed to his left arm. I must admit that I was distracted, and emotional. Events momentous in our lives were running past me like water down a mill-race, totally out of my control. Once again, in my heart, I knew that a chapter in our lives was ending. I seized my cane and hurried out and leaned on the terrace balustrade. The general and his horse were motionless as he watched the hussars move into column. On a heedless impulse, I raised my cane and shouted, 'Vive l'Empereur!' As one, Bertrand and every hussar in the detachment drew their sabres with an emphatic clashing of steel and the raucous chorus came back: 'Vive l'Empereur!' I felt my face warm in gratification. The next moment they were trotting away up the drive amid the cheers and clapping of the population of 'Chanson'. Therese now stood on the terrace, supported by her servants, waving her thin arm. She continued to wave until the party was long out of sight. It is a vision of her which will remain with me until the day I die.

Pierre told himself: The true emotions of an honest and humane man. He felt warmth in his own face. He read on. The entries during the following month were few, and commonplace. The saddle-maker had the bottles with the preserving spirit, destined never to be used, taken away. Madame Montmorency wrote to tell him that her son had escaped to Boston, in America, and was starting a wine business importing from the family's estate in Bordeaux. Anton recorded his immense relief, and wished the young fellow well. Of course, the atmosphere at 'Chanson' was tense, awaiting news on the military situation. On 12 June, a letter from the general arrived for Therese, the saddle-maker noted, but did not say whether his wife had told him anything of its contents. So probably she hadn't. The *Moniteur* reported the Grande Armée's movements in Prussia – avidly studied by Anton. The saddle-maker's business thrived – like the Emperor's fortunes – at its zenith. As he acknowledged to himself, they were irrevocably linked. His surgeon came and went, attending to Therese. At her invitation, he continued to take tea with her each afternoon, and the children spent the half-hour with them. 'I believe her intention is for me to become better acquainted with our children', he wrote.

His child and Bertrand's! She knows what is coming, Pierre thought. He stood up for one of his stretches. What he did have as a legacy from his army national service, thirty years ago, aggravated by long hours at his computer, was a troublesome back. He'd served in an airborne regiment and completed fifty-one jumps, some less successful than others, including a landing on a moving armoured vehicle – that was the root of the problem. He walked across the salon. A film of dust adhered to table-tops. Madame Roget is to return in a few days.

His forebear was weighed down with premonitions of what waited in ambush in his household's future: Therese on her sick-bed, the general journeying to yet another sanguinary encounter, the somewhat belated worry now gnawing in his innards regarding the children's situation. Yet, he had an ability to bounce back to equilibrium even in the face of the harshest realities. Anton, the survivor.

Pierre walked to a window, gazed out and pondered this. Notwithstanding, had Anton run to the limits of his measured self-sufficiency? He'd written, in characters thicker-inked than usual, perhaps indicating heightened emotion: 'I am conscious that I have no more power over my life's direction than leaves in an autumn storm'.

Leaves, in an autumn storm – the persons in the journal, the characters in his novel to be, were just that. Pierre surmised if the saddle-maker might, at this time of great personal trouble, have also applied the heartfelt analogy to the wider spectrum: a nation being swept along in the wind of one man's overriding and terrific ambition. The journal, however, had been devoid of political opinions; even with level-headed, humane Anton, his business pragmatism appeared to have come up trumps. Rumours were in the air, he noted, of a great battle fought at Friedland.

It was after 2 p.m. Pierre felt hungry. He went out to the kitchen and cut into the crusty loaf, then into a block of cheddar cheese, and made a sandwich. The afternoon sun flooded into the salon, and he blinked as he returned to his chair. Earlier, he'd riffled the remaining unread pages. An hour's read, unless he ran into something that stopped him in his tracks; he was on the edge of entering the territory of the blueprint and the continuum that he'd assigned to the Prince of Imagination to work on. This nocturnal decision which he'd made the other night, as he'd brewed coffee, had vexed him as to whether it was the correct path for the narrative. It was. He must break away from Anton, and begin a new journey.

Therese and Bertrand were going to die; that seemed self-evident to the novelist. Events, irrevocably, were weighted toward it. After their deaths, the blueprint in his head had Anton fading from the scene, and Pierre would let him go.

At 2.30 p.m., he was back in his chair. The salon windows were wide open to admit a refreshing breeze.

Pierre realised that he was breathing a little faster.

'Chanson', 18 June 1807

I was visiting one of my farms when a groom from the
stables galloped up with an urgent message from my
housekeeper. Hurriedly, I returned in the landau. The
two hussar officers who had been here a month since
were waiting. The campaign chest was also in the hall.
A pain gripped my heart. Here was a mute declaration
of tragic news. As I pen these words, at midnight,
my emotion is more constrained – even so, I will not
attempt to convey other than a bare outline of what next
occurred. There is no doubt in my mind that Therese
had long since prepared herself for this tragic event – as
had I. In our thoughts, rehearsals of this moment had
been endured. When I entered her apartment, my dear
wife, pale and strained with anxiety, studied my face,
then turned her own to the wall; I assume that she
heard my quiet words, although she made no response,
either by voice or gesture. There was no out-pouring
of grief, just silence. Her personal maid sat with me
by her bed all day. She took no sustenance except
for a few sips of water. As the evening shadows crept
across the room, at the end of that brilliant summer
day, she murmured to her maid; her small daughter was
brought in, she cradled her and we heard faint soothing
whispers. At about 8 p.m., her maid requested me to
leave. Marcel was waiting outside the door and he led
me to the dining room. This is not usually part of his
duties; no doubt he had been instructed to watch over
me. He sat outside the dining room door while they
brought me dinner. I ate slowly, gazing at the candle-
light flickering on the dark-panelled wall – as if in a

valedictory tribute to the life that the three of us have known. That notion came to me. Naturally, my thoughts were upstairs with Therese; and with our friend, the general, wherever he lay in East Prussia. His officers said that he will be re-interred at Paris's Cimetière du Père Lachaise; that the officers of the brigade are subscribing to a monument. I was informed that he died a heroic and instant death, charging at the head of his brigade. He was fifty-one years old. No other details were offered, or needed, although I may read more in the *Moniteur*. I called Marcel in, and invited him to drink a toast with me. Of course, we drank Chambertin. We stood side-by-side. 'To the memory of Brigadier-General Bertrand, commander of the 3rd Brigade of Hussars, a valiant officer of the Empire. *Vive l'Empereur!*', I said, and we drank. Marcel was quite affected. Since our Prussian adventure, he has been more withdrawn than usual. I fear that the form of the words I used was incorrect, but I am unpractised in such matters. I went back to spend the night in an armchair outside Therese's apartment, praying I would not be called, but fearing that I might be. Yes, praying … although my past study of religion was an incoherent mass in my mind. One might ask where our priest has been in our tribulations. Well, he was here, at last, this afternoon, praying by her bed. My surgeon will come at day-break. He is as exhausted as any one of us. I must see that his devotion is well rewarded.

Pierre brooded on the crisis described. The saddle-maker's calm prose had soothed his earlier tension. He was conscious that the saga – so far as the journal was concerned – was nearly over. There was only one more entry to read, dated 27 June. He felt that the narrative had been relentlessly heading towards this juncture: a painful and bitter cross-roads in their lives. Bertrand had been on borrowed time for years, and Therese's life-force seemed to have been that of a day-lily. He'd been peering into lives poised on a knife-edge. Only Anton seemed to have durability.

Under the shower this morning, in his mind the blueprint had been projected on the white tiles. The novel's structure was there; however, so were significant gaps – the details as to how certain linkages could be made to work were yet to emerge from his unconscious. The two new characters were fairly clear to him … All of his preparatory reading of the saddle-maker's journal, the research material, had to be put behind him, his imagination let loose. He must shift into campaign mode, as did the Emperor when the periods of mobilising resources, the political and strategic manoeuvring, were completed. He stood a long time under the hot water, various thoughts streaming through his mind as the water streamed off his head. Remember, he told himself, history can be slipperier than fiction.

A strong breeze sallied out from the Jardin des Plantes, as if making a break for the streets and boulevards, on its way rattling the doors and windows of the salon. Pierre took up the journal for 1807 and, with a tension in his own chest, addressed the final entry.

'Chanson', 27 June 1807
It is now eight days since my dear and lovely Therese passed away. I cannot write of my grief, only say that I have come through these days as if sleep-walking.

My servants have been a wonderful support with the
necessary arrangements, and quite unexpectedly,
Madame Montmorency and Madame Rey visited me,
and were most helpful in certain matters. Otherwise,
at all hours I have walked the rooms and corridors
of my beloved 'Chanson' and, without exaggeration,
I believe I can say that during these broken-hearted
perambulations a soft and quite cheerful song has been
in my mind. In these hours, my last vision of her has
been fixed in my head: on her bed, the fine hairs on her
arms, the fine, still-blue veins, the face sad yet peaceful.
The children, I suspect, are too young to understand
the tragedy that has come down on us. Nevertheless,
they must be missing their mother in ways that I
cannot fathom, although they play quietly together. I
am spending an hour with them each day at their tea-
time. The servants are taking their usual attentive care.
Her jewellery, and intimate and valuable possessions,
including letters, have been sent into safe custody for
her daughter. I added to this the letter which arrived
from him, three days after she passed away. Naturally, it
remains sealed. In my study, as I write this, her shawl,
and his sabre are before my eyes. They will be put safely
aside for her daughter, and my son … I must write this:
My dear wife, consumed by her passions, could no
more brook them than the leaves on our oak trees can
resist the autumn winds tugging them into their dying
descent. And, she loved us all.

In my heart, the white roses sent to me from time to
time are no longer a mystery.
God in his mercy lend her grace.

My heart is broken. This is my last entry.

Pierre sits at his corner table in the restaurant on the Boulevard St-Germain and contemplates the deep ruby colour of the wine. Thank God, the tension in his chest has gone; now he feels drained, exhausted. It seems to him that, in alternate bouts, the story has been charging him up with energy or sucking it out. Now, at the end, it's downside. Anton's last written words are haunting his mind. The meaning of the periodic gifts of white roses from his beloved Therese, somewhat strange in the circumstances finally, was clear to the saddle-maker; yet, he was enigmatic about it. So, what illumination had he received?

Pierre stares at the red wine as if mesmerised, meditates on the question … Delicate little messages of affection – and gratitude – from a tortured soul?

He nods to himself. It is his best guess.

Monsieur Jacques comes to the table, bringing – at the novelist's invitation – another glass. The proprietor fills it from the bottle on the side-table, and waits. Pierre stands up, glass in hand and lifts it to eye-level, twirls it. Almost like fire-light, the discreet lighting dances in the liquid. Monsieur Jacques, in anticipation, also raises his glass.

Pierre intones for their ears only: 'To my forebear, Anton Brun, in memory of his extraordinary character and loving devotion to his wife, Therese'.

They drink. In Pierre's mouth, the wine is superbly con-centrated, generous and bright. True to form, Monsieur Jacques' face remains expressionless, as they stand together for a few moments, then he bows to the eccentric novelist for whom he has friendly feelings, and retreats to his cubby-hole.

Pierre resumes his seat. Paul, the star chef, is cooking tonight. He's ordered *entrecôte à la bordelaise*. Suddenly he has an appetite. The groundwork for his new novel is laid, but he's going to miss his forebear's intimacies, more than he can presently imagine.

Tonight, he's worn a homburg bought in London, carries a stick with a mother-of-pearl inlaid handle, and is slightly amused to observe the reverential way the old, foot-sore waiter bears them away.

Intruding into his thoughts: a familiar laugh. He turns in his chair. From another corner, Lucile is smiling across the room at him. She nods slightly, as though approving of the small piece of theatre that she's just witnessed, though she cannot know what it meant. She is with a male companion of urbane appearance, who is also looking Pierre over.

Dear Reader, for a brief space, I choose to again step forward. Take off my invisible cloak? Pierre would like that notion. The re-appearance of the green-eyed Lucile – thank heavens she now has a name – has a significance, to be revealed later. In his past fictions, Pierre uses this little trick of the trade: planting a clue to a future development. Or, at a telling moment, he remains silent. In the latter, he is under the influence of his mentor John Fowles, who famously said: 'One of the greatest arts of the novel is omission – leaving it to the reader's imagination to do the work'.

I am inclined to humour Pierre's mini-conceits regarding his princes of this and that – they don't too much get under my feet. The same goes for his dress-ups *à l auteur* with his street clothes, which he makes out to be a bit of personal comedy – though is that a self-delusion? I'm sure that bits and pieces of the person he sees himself to be are that. Further, while I'm in control of some sections of his novels, he has his own precincts and sometimes it's a bit of a tug-of-war.

Pierre will soon reveal the details that he's been holding back of the blueprint, from after the journal period – in effect, his main turning point. Thereafter, I will throw in one of my own, which will parallel his story. He'll mostly likely never learn of mine, except by an accident, thus it won't be in his finished novel.

'For heaven's sake!', you complain.

I respond: 'Look at it this way: it'll be part of the story that is there but off the page; really, out of the novel, existing in a parallel world, for you to imagine, if you so choose'.

Smoke and mirrors? You're dead right. Let's see if I can do it.

Finally, the business of Pierre's rubbing his scar, and reflecting on his wife's untimely and tragic death, are others of his hints, and I rather doubt whether he will explain them much more – either because he's following Fowles's precept, or because it's just too distressing for him. I think that I should lay it out on his behalf. Possibly, you've approximately guessed what happened. He ran his car into a tree one night when he'd been drinking. She died. He'll never get over it. He went to prison for eighteen months. Guilt remains with him: a slow-burn. But he wears a good mask. There you are.

The next morning, Pierre woke to sounds in the kitchen. Madame Roget was back! A half-hour later, ablutions completed, he was sitting in the sunshine on the balcony eating the croissant, and sipping her fragrant coffee. On entering the kitchen, he'd greeted her with a handshake and a few words of welcome. Unexpectedly, she was dressed in a floral dress, covered by her usual apron. He'd anticipated more sombre attire, even black; it appeared, however, despite her bereavement, that she was joining in with spring. She'd even parted with a brief smile. 'The temperature is going up now', she said. And it was.

He nodded at the white rose, still dewy, in a specimen vase on the table. 'Thank you. It's lovely.'

'From my sister's garden.'

White roses ... the interlude last night, at Monsieur Jacques' restaurant, was a kind of valedictory occasion to mark the end of the *ménage à trois*, and the saddle-maker's noble conduct throughout those years, which was Pierre's firm opinion on that. All of it might have been a dream in the sledge-bed. It wasn't, nor was the presence of Lucile at the restaurant.

Paris, at its heart, is a relatively small city and walking home he'd thought over this most recent brief encounter. She and her companion had departed unobtrusively, without even exchanging a greeting; only her smile, her look. He supposed that she mightn't have wished to intrude on this eccentric novelist's mysterious little ceremony, his introverted brooding. 'Or, maybe your goose is cooked', he'd murmured to the spring evening, thinking of her urbane dinner companion.

He left the balcony, and went to the salon and his reading chair. He sat, and gazed to the far end of the room. The blueprint, which had evolved in sessions under the rose-head shower's downpour, was up on his mental screen; not a word of it was down on paper. Right at this moment, the two new protagonists in the story of Anton, Therese and Brigadier-General Bertrand were having their breakfasts in provincial towns, far apart. A man and a woman, in their fifties, unknown to each other, who'd been spawned in his unconscious to renew the love story, carry it on – descendants of the two children born at 'Chanson'. The continuum.

Pierre brushed his scar. He'd thought hard about bringing in a researcher (as the saddle-maker had done with his Paris agent, when he'd been tracking down the miscreant officers) to trace Anton's genealogy, then abandoned the idea. Whether the boy and girl had survived, or whether a line of descent had eventuated, was immaterial to his purposes. He would move beyond the confines of historical record into the new territory that the Prince of Imagination was reconnoitring; go through Fowles' door; break outside the square – just as Bertrand, the cavalryman, had in his battlefield tactics, galloping free of the staid infantry squares. He'd move into his domain: fiction.

He told himself: you could say it a dozen ways, and maybe none of them will make sense. Yet in recent days, he'd been imagining the man and woman, could see their faces, hear their voices, feel these fictional creations brushing past his body.

But, he had to find the way to get it straight in his head, and down on paper. He was leaping beyond his previous experience and achievements. There were gaps in the blueprint, a host of questions still to answer. How were these new lovers to meet? How much did they know of their heritage – if anything? If nothing, what explanation could be devised for the drifting apart of the two lines of descent, over the intervening two hundred years? How would they fall in love? He, a retired bank manager, widowed like himself; she, a high school principal, a widow – was that stretching it too far? Imagined people waiting to be lovers, nevertheless, becoming as real to him as those below his windows walking in the Jardin des Plantes. But, above all, had they inherited knowledge of the existence of Therese and Bertrand – and Anton – and of their convoluted love?

For most of the morning, Pierre pondered these questions, and others. What had happened to the saddle-maker's collections of butterflies, and clocks? If they'd survived, they might have come down to the bank manager and the school mistress. As for 'Chanson', it also might feature in lore passed down. And, a portrait of Therese, if one existed, could hang in one or other of their houses. It didn't need to've been an actuality for him to use it. The Prince of Co-incidence was mincing down a corridor in his mind, throwing up the slippery possibilities. The image of the sabre that he'd viewed in the auction house was before him. Anton had kept the sabre, and the shawl, to pass down to the children; in his blueprint, his new fictional characters, through their forebears, had them. Between the two new lovers, any one of these things could bridge a connection.

He paced the salon, thinking about his next move. He decided, went to the telephone and made a call. A conversation ensued and he returned to the salon, nodding to himself rather warily; the appointment at 3 p.m. would confirm whether he'd made a right move, in more ways than one.

An early lunch on the balcony followed, during which he was thinking – as he ate the salmon quiche – not of the forthcoming appointment, but beyond it. Without consulting him, Madame Roget poured a glass of delicate yet straightforward Sancerre; right in tune with his mood.

Lucile was waiting in the hall of the small suburban museum when he arrived at a few minutes to three. He crossed the marble floor to her. Today it was a red straw hat fixed to the side of her head, a red cotton dress, sleeveless. His eye fell on her bare arms; they were speckled with sunspots and interesting small imperfections. She smiled at his intent gaze.

'Thank you for this', he said.

After his briefing on the phone, she'd suggested this venue as a possible solution. She'd said: 'Would you like me to do research on the internet? I could e-mail you the results.' He'd replied: 'I don't have e-mail'. Five years ago he'd cancelled his account, sick of the life and distractions that it brought to him – his reclusive phase, and he'd kept it up, which might've been a reason that his agent had dropped out of the loop. All round, he'd been going for the semi-reclusive life. In his own way, with his retreats to 'Chanson', and lack of friends, hadn't Anton been following the same path?

'They could have something on the second floor', she said.

The shawls, in silk, lace, wool and cashmere, from Persia and the Far East, were displayed in many glass cases. 'Belgium is over here', she pointed with the arm that was fascinating him.

He gazed into the display case. Circa early nineteenth century, a card noted. Longer than he'd imagined, almost dress-length, the lace of an intricate pattern – 'Flemish bobbin-lace', the card read. He mused on it. It was merely an example of the period. Probably, Therese's had been different, so why the need to see one? His imagination would've done duty.

Head slightly to one side, she was watching his reaction. 'Is it a key item in your story?'

He thought a moment, then looked up. 'The novel's title is *The Sabre and the Shawl*. I've seen the sabre – I think a pretty good example of what's in the story – but the shawl isn't described in detail. It's a bit mysterious in that respect, which fits the character of the woman it was presented to in 1806. No, not a key part of the story, but I wanted to see one, to complete the link.'

'I take it we're talking about a person who existed?'

'Yes, most of the characters will be based on real people … Not all.'

This would do. He took a final look, and they moved away.

But, one more thing. He turned to this green-eyed woman. 'It was presented by a Brigadier-General Hubert Bertrand, to a Madame Therese Brun.'

'It's a love story', she said quietly, as if to herself, then: 'That'll be a first for you. I've read all your books.'

He gives her the smile derided by the actress: 'Time for a change'.

He is dressed casually in a suede bomber-jacket, and is hatless. It's the kind of gear he'd put a certain character into. A character he doesn't quite trust. He's fantasising, he knows, yet today maybe he's trying to give her a different impression of himself than hitherto; with her, check his status.

She couldn't stop for coffee. A lady of appointments,

he thinks. He watches her cross the pavement and hail a taxi. The interlude in Monsieur Jacques' restaurant, which has been on his mind as having significance, hasn't come up, and perhaps never will. Well, he's given her a glimpse into his workaday world, if you can call it that. Whether the move has been right or wrong is still an open question. Possibly, she's gone off for a late-afternoon rendezvous with the urbane erstwhile dinner companion; on Pierre Brun's part, any moves now are too late.

Pierre flexes his shoulders, walks across a small park; she has gone and he is missing her. Disturbing ... He looks at the beds of spring flowers that he is passing. Abruptly, a picture of the vegetable garden that he'd tended at the prison is also back, superimposed on the municipal garden. A shred of memory; he'd been on auto-pilot throughout that time – probably that had got him through. Now he shrugs, shifts his mind back to the novel. The shawl rates a bit higher than he's admitted to her. The gift from Bertrand had been a token of love, had emerged from the surprising, sensitive side of his personality; that, and a handful of his other recorded caring gestures, stood in stark contrast – it had to be said – to the sabre, a symbol of his killer's trade, and life. Every novel should have a symbol or two, so long as they stood up to the light of day. One that in a midnight writing stint was as black as the ace of spades, could look pretty wan in the cold light of dawn. He stood on a corner. Voice of experience. The depression that the journal had been holding at bay was circling. He felt uncomfortable in the ultra-casual clothes; with his understanding of Therese, and the green-eyed Lucile; with his ability to write the novel – any novel. 'To hell with these moods which swing from pole to pole', he mutters.

At 5 p.m., Pierre was back in his salon, standing at the window, cup of tea in hand, looking across the gardens and roof-tops, to the distant dome of the Hôtel des Invalides, golden in the fading sunlight. Madame Roget had brought him a small danish pastry, with blackberry jam, that he'd eaten with relish. With such a concession to his diabetes, things were looking up. Maybe tomorrow morning, he could expect two croissants on the breakfast table. He grins; he's swinging back to the other pole.

However, it was inconsequential thoughts of this nature that were postponing his confrontation with the computer keyboard. Once he'd finished reading the journal, assembling his blueprint, his intention had been to begin writing. It hadn't happened. The structured reading had kept him on course, now he was adrift with questions on the way ahead bumping through his mind like unclaimed luggage on a conveyor belt. If only he could grab one piece and begin unpacking it, he'd have a start! Sure, in his head, he'd worked out the blueprint – up to a point – nonetheless, black on white wasn't happening.

'I'm just kicking the can down the road, like the bloody politicians with the European Union debt disaster', he murmured to the mellow evening that cared nothing for the Global Financial Crisis. He thought: God, I'll be watching television again any day.

His two characters, in their provincial towns, were fretting to be on their way into the story. He truly felt that. He wasn't ready, and from past experience he knew that it would be counter-productive to push it. And now another mini road-block, harnessed with lights, was flickering in his mind: the Cimetière du Père Lachaise – the famous cemetery, where the general, presumably, was interred.

113

He remembered the scene in the hall at 'Chanson', when the hussar officers had informed the saddle-maker of the memorial to be erected by the officers of his brigade. This was where the new characters would meet! If he could ever get them there!

The next morning, Pierre was outside the cemetery's white stone gates when they opened. Sunshine was about, but also intermittent showers that had washed the city's morning face. He felt buoyant with expectation: another box in his blueprint was going to be ticked. Also, it had been a two-croissant breakfast. Briskly, he walked up the avenue from the gates. It was like a city within a city, he reflected: a final home for a million citizens, or three million if those cremated were counted. He'd found the location of Bertrand's monument on the website. It wasn't far from the gate; the brigadier-general had been an early-bird in this cemetery.

Here we are, he thought. Marvellous! The officers had dug deep in their purses, perhaps thoughtful of their own precarious mortality. An edifice in white stone, with inlaid panels of greyish marble, encrusted with ornament surmounting its top, carved in relief in its base: horses, drums, standards, swords, trumpets. Bertrand's name, rank and decorations cut into a marble scroll. All of it flecked with raindrops from the passing showers.

He stared, taking in the detail, bit by bit. It struck him that it had the dead-weight heaviness of a cavalry charge, or the ponderosity of the Emperor's conquering ambitions. Yet it matched only one side – the obvious one – of Bertrand's character.

Pierre stepped back a few paces, and on the far side of the monument he saw the low marble slab with a modest raised headstone. Breathing a little faster, he walked around to it. He stared at the elegantly chiselled text:

THERESE MARIA BRUN. BELOVED WIFE OF ANTON BRUN

DEVOTED MOTHER OF HENRI AND ANGELIQUE

DEAR FRIEND OF HUBERT BERTRAND

AT PEACE, AMID THE STARS.

Pierre exhales his breath. This is down to his forebear, the saddle-maker to the Emperor. He is shaken. He gazes at the small, delicate tribute to the chatelaine of 'Chanson'. Beside the solid-grounded, grandiloquent other it seems to hover, ethereal as a wisp of cloud.

Why such a shock? Isn't this the final noble gesture that he should've expected from Anton?

Pierre turns on his heel and walks back toward the gates, almost in a dream. He has not thought ahead as to where she might be interred. Outside the gate, he purchases flowers and returns to the two monuments. Again it begins to sprinkle rain. Bending down, he lays the six white roses in a line abreast under her name. In a moment, they are dewy with raindrops.

Pierre leaves the famous cemetery and goes to the café nearest the gates. He has settled down. The anticipatory excitement that he'd arrived with, the subsequent shock, have been supplanted by an uplifting glow of warm satisfaction. He stands inside the door of the café and surveys the establishment: a film director looking, for the first time, on a set for a key scene?

That is what he's doing. The café will be the set for his novel's climactic scene. Somehow, it's to be the place where the man and the woman from the provincial towns will meet. It's in the blueprint. One can describe them as his distant cousins, even though they are creations of his imagination. He waves a waiter away.

'Somehow', that's the operative word. What will prompt them to come here? What piece of plot can he find to make it work?

He takes a few paces into the interior and looks around, drinking in the physical features, the atmosphere. Really, it's a pretty ordinary café. On the wall near the door is a placard. He glances at it, his eyes move on, then switch back. Below artwork of cannons and standards, it says: 'Société de la Grande Armée. During the month of June, the Society, on the dates given, will commemorate the anniversaries of the deaths of the following heroic officers.' There are two names, and one is *chef de brigade*, Hubert Bertrand.

Wondering at his quicksilver morning, the novelist walks out of the café and down the Rue du Repos. A crucial missing part of his plot, a vacant box on the blueprint, has been filled in. It's time for a drink – a morning for a glass of Chambertin, if he can find a place around here which serves it – and a ham and cheese baguette. Suddenly he is hungry.

The other tomb which he'd had a quick look at in passing was that of Marshal Murat, the legendary chief of cavalry.

Bertrand must have known him and they lay not twenty metres apart now. He wondered if the brigadier-general had ever had a conversation with that magnificent personage, though, of course, conversation wasn't Bertrand's strong-point. He smiled; you could say that the cemetery, virtually, was garrisoned by the Emperor's marshals and generals.

Dear Reader, only a brief appearance, as I'm wont to say. I think you should know this: right now, we are going to leave Pierre. I'm not sidelining him; it's more a bit of by-passing. I wish to push the narrative ahead to its conclusion. He'll be back, because the finale will be all his, as at last he sits down 'to put black on white' – using his cliché'd phrase. Of course, when he does, he might decide to sideline me, by cunningly moving into a first-person narrative. However, I don't think so, as he's never done such before. Good God! – he and the saddle-maker, working side-by-side, as 'I'? That's headache territory. Anyway, when he does commence the writing, I'll be at his elbow, inside his head, in his dreams, in his unconscious – whatever you like – plying my omniscient narrator's trade.

He's gone further with the 'new' story than I expected; his Prince of Imagination hasn't let him down. But I'm about to reveal the actual onward story – the continuum – that'll parallel it, though I'm not sure 'parallel' is quite right. Pierre might or might not learn about it. Either way, it won't matter. I believe that his imagination will create a story independent of this reality, this knowledge. Confusing? Doubtless it is, but I'm inviting you to imagine what may be happening, off the edge of the page. Pretentious twaddle? So what? Remember John Fowles' dictum? Pierre and I subscribe to that.

So far, we've had a *mélange* of intrusions: his wife's tragic death; his prison time; his procrastination over a new woman; the by-play with his housekeeper; his ruminations on the writing life and search for an 'ignition point'; and, of course, his reading of Anton's journal, and subsequent puzzlement about the saddle-maker's character and motives. Fair enough. He's trying to decide what to put in, and how to write his novel, attempting to break out of his barren period. Writer's block is not a myth.

I'm not a slave to deadlines, but my magazine is gasping for financial oxygen and this moonlighting risks knocking it into a cocked hat. Come to think of it, Pierre has never met a deadline in his life.

Thus I must hasten. The coming two wedges of narrative will be brief.

Henri Brun's story: At his dinner table, Henri – retired bank manager and resident of Strasbourg, aged fifty-seven, widower for three years, childless – was enjoying the *veau sauté marengo* that he'd cooked. It was after 8 p.m., and with the tradesman-like skills that he'd taught himself during his wife's long illness, he'd prepared the dish with some finesse: the veal lightly fried in oil with onion and tomato, and separately, the mushrooms, then sprinkled with flour, a bit of wine and stock, clove of garlic, and a slow-cook for an hour or so. He'd found the recipe in a restaurant in Vendée. He had *France Soir* propped up, the front page at eye-level, and between precise mouthfuls he scanned the leading news feature. He read and listened to music, at his mostly solitary meals. A tall but slight man, with a high, receding brow, face mottled with brown ageing marks, and thin, sandy hair, he was dressed in immaculate casual clothes. An orderly, disciplined individual, his life had become even more precise following his wife's death, as if remembering her adjunct not to let his standards slip – though in the beginning, he had. His sister had come to stay for a while, and pulled him out of that decline. Those, also, had been his standards at the bank, until he'd taken an early-retirement package. His house was one of those narrow, tall manifestations of the city's history, built on a cobbled street fronting the river. He didn't know how long he'd have the endurance to make it up the steep staircase to his bedroom, but at present it wasn't a problem. He ate slowly, savouring the flavours in the dish. He turned over the front page of the famous Paris evening newspaper and folded it down. Schubert's Fourth came softly from the radio. The Sèvres blue porcelain clock ticked delicate, spring-time sounds. He was analysing the moment, the atmosphere – one of his habits. The colour photograph of the Cimetière du Père Lachaise claimed his attention. A surprise; it was a destination that he was planning to go to – a plan, following certain discoveries that he'd made in recent weeks. His eyes drifted down the newsprint columns, stopped at the last paragraph, an endnote: 'Brigadier-General Hubert Bertrand …' He put his knife and fork together on the plate, and still reading leaned forward in his chair. 'Société de la Grande Armée: this month, a ceremony to commemorate the anniversary of the death of this Napoleonic cavalry *chef de brigade* will be held at the Cemetery.' The former banker stood up, left the dining room, and went into the corridor. In the hall, on a marble-topped, wrought-iron-framed table, a porcelain vase, placed beside his wife's photograph, displayed blue and white blooms, her favourite colours; on the wall above, in a long glass case, the venerable sabre inherited from his father was mounted. He studied it anew: no over-elaborate gilding or decoration, not a ceremonial weapon, just a plain cavalryman's battle-scarred cutting tool that, two hundred years ago, had belonged to the hussar, Bertrand, and until recently had merely been an anonymous icon on the wall. Henri had only had this information for about a month; in that period, his and his family's past had taken on a new dimension. The heart-attack that he'd survived six months ago, and the task of clearing out a deceased bachelor ex-colleague's house – he'd been named as executor – had presaged the change, put him onto a new course, into a period of introspection about his own life, and possessions. Dealing with the colleague's lifetime accumulation of the latter had horrified and exhausted Henri, and he'd resolved not to impose such an ordeal on his executor; thus the foray into his own attic, and the discovery of the faded packet of sixteen letters penned by Madame Therese Brun, of 'Chanson' (as the letterhead proclaimed), between 1805 and May 1807 (the last) to the brigadier-general, addressed to many different destinations. When he'd taken the packet from the steel box, a faint perfume had come to him (the perfume of Therese Brun?); in seconds, it evaporated. He'd always had a taste for history, and he'd read and re-read the letters, avidly. He'd surmised that they were the surviving fragment of a larger correspondence. Therese's writing style was both breathless, then, in turn, measured and thoughtful. He'd decided: a character with surface shine, and also solemn depths. Certain of her paragraphs were immediately fixed in his mind. Henri had a photographic memory, much to the trepidation of his subordinates at the bank. In April 1807, she'd written:

My Dearest,

I am consumed with my fears for your safety, and have hardly slept since we parted, and then heard that war is imminent. My dear love, why must you keep returning to the places of greatest danger? You have served the Emperor so long, so dutifully, so bravely, has not the time come for rest and repose, and enjoyment of whatever life may remain to us? And, of course, I make this plea also for our dearest child. Forgive me, Dearest, for my entreaties. I cannot ignore the emotions welling in my heart …

The passionate nature still breathed from the faded blue pages. How had the battle-scarred, veteran cavalryman responded to words like this? Henri wondered. The soldier must have been something, to inspire such love and devotion. He thirsted to have the other side of the correspondence, did not expect to ever have it. But he'd found 'Chanson', with the aid of a real estate agent whom he knew through the bank, and had visited the crumbling château, now circumscribed by a modern suburb. He'd wandered around the creeper-entwined walls, puzzling over what part the place had held in their lives. The property had been owned by Anton Brun, doubtless his ancestor, though as yet he'd found out little about him. His was a shadowy figure behind the lovers, though a clue came from several references in Therese's letters:

Dearest, my dear constant husband is as
thoughtful and considerate to my needs as a
person could be – our needs, I should say – and
from your words, I know you acknowledge our
indebtedness to him. He is a true friend to us
both, and 'Chanson' is now the home that you
have never had …

Henri thought: If the general was something, then Anton
Brun certainly was, too. He'd walked along the river,
musing over the letters, and the story partly revealed: a
memorable affair. He returned to the dining room, carried
his plate out to the kitchen and placed it in the dishwasher.
Then he went back, with another glass of the Vouvray that
he'd been drinking, and stared again at the sabre. Well, the
days of glory and heartache had passed away. He'd found a
reference, a few weeks ago, to the number of wounds that
Bertrand had suffered. One tally gave them as fifteen. At
the end, the poor fellow must have been a stiff, tottering
testimony to them, and to the hard weather of campaigns.
His own city of Strasbourg, and Alsace, had provided the
French Revolution with sixty-four marshals and generals,
many of whom had served the Emperor. 'I have been
stabbed by your beloved dagger a thousand times, my love,
and I treasure the memories of my wounds, just as my
fingers worship the scars on your beloved body.' Reading
these words, Henri had nodded to himself; the other part
of the essence, the raunchy one, of the fragile, fine-spun
Therese he imagined, but fine-spun steel, too. He went
to his study on the first floor, up the creaking stairs, the
gurgling river-sounds coming in the open windows, and

took out the railway timetable. He'd intended to go to the Cimetière du Père Lachaise, and now he would on that special day. Since his heart-turn, he'd diligently followed his doctor's instructions on diet and exercise, and felt much healthier. In fact, he felt as if he were on the edge of a new step in his life. It's not over yet, he told himself.

Angelique Bertrand's story: Angelique, recently retired librarian, aged fifty-five, never married (not Pierre's fictional construct, who is a school principal and widow), friend of many, life-long resident of Lyons, is a woman of exquisite talents and taste (for instance, her embroidery is celebrated among her friends, and decorates many of their tea-tables, the blue and gold flowers, and motifs, a sun-warmed delight to beholders). She is a trained researcher, with a penchant for local history, although lately, local history has been put aside for a focused delving into her family's provenance. (We will come to that shortly.) She is a tall, long-striding, lithesome woman, with auburn hair worn in what is perhaps an old-fashioned French-roll, very fair in her complexion, a good regional cook (Curnonsky's famous book is her bible), altogether a bit over-the-top in her accomplishments and persona, which some have surmised frightened off a number of suitors in her younger days. Yet she is a quiet and serious person, possessed of another exquisite quality: a delightful – understated – sense of humour. Above all, she is a happy and contented individual, very comfortable in her religion. This morning, she has been preparing for a small dinner party – I will spare you further descriptions of food and cooking that Pierre is addicted to – but she stopped when the friends telephoned to send their regrets; a venerable aunt in Dijon has been taken ill. So she has a free day that she'll devote to her project. Last night, she read *France Soir* and the article on the Cimetière du Père Lachaise, with its mention of the brigadier-general. It isn't news to her that he's interred there (though she hasn't yet visited his tomb), but it is that there's to be a commemorative ceremony in five days. Her grandmother, and mother, passed down parts of the story of Therese and the general, and since she's had the time, she's found out a good deal more, and even a certain amount about the enigmatic Anton Brun; she knows that he was a prominent supplier of saddles to the Emperor. But it is her fresh contemplation of the inherited items in her own household that is intriguing her: the Belgian shawl, the packet of the general's letters, the medium-sized portrait of Therese that has hung in the drawing room of her house all her remembered life – the house had been her mother's. (More of this in a moment …) In her efficient way, she has transcribed into typescript the dozen dirt-stained letters, sent from battlefields and Continental nations, and the cavalryman's emotion-challenged sentences lie in her mind as heavy as musket balls. In 1806, he wrote:

My dearest love,

I note with a heavy heart your entreaties. I wish I could reply in a manner that would assuage your fears, but I am a person who has formed his life around the Emperor's great and noble ambitions for our nation. Honour and duty run through my veins with my blood, and I cannot break the mould. You, of all persons, know how difficult it is for me to find words to express my thoughts and feelings … It is my nature, but also the influence

of my profession. I hope you, and our beloved
daughter, will forgive me …

The last letter in the packet has not been unsealed. On the
envelope, it is dated 10 June 1807. She has debated with
herself whether to open it, and will not – yet, anyway – as
she understands that both the lovers were dead when it
was delivered. For the present, she wishes to preserve its
mystery. Behind its unsealed state, she senses the intent
and thoughts of Anton Brun. If only she had Therese's! She
longs to hear the voice of her ancestor. Now she goes into
the drawing room, and stands before Therese. In recent
times, the portrait has become a shrine in her house,
brought forward from its long, semi-neglected sojourn. The
lovely flesh-tones of the liberally exposed neck and bosom,
the wispy greys and blues of her gown, the sapphires in the
necklace, the pensive expression, as if she is at a moment
of introspection (on her life and times?) – a loving,
sympathetic look in the luminous green eyes – and, the
fine auburn hair (an unknown particular to our novelist,
Pierre!). 'An ethereal angel', Angelique whispers to herself,
as she has before. There is no artist's signature, no date, no
words on the reverse, but she feels almost certain that it was
commissioned by her shadowy husband, not by the general.
It is a morning for this. She goes upstairs to her bedroom,
running her hand up the shining mahogany banister,
polished a thousand times by her mother, herself. There she
opens the bottom drawer of an oak chest. The crisp layers
of tissue-paper crackle, and whisper, like a long-forgotten
narrative coming to light, as she lifts out the package, lays
it on her bed, and folds them back. For perhaps the fifth or
sixth time in the past month, she admires, with her skilled

eye, the Belgian shawl, reputedly bought by the general in a German town for his paramour. 'Ah', she sighs; it is all a wonder. Of course, she will go to Paris for the ceremony; in the background, she will revel quietly in the occasion.

This morning, Pierre felt a little nervous in the stomach, though he'd breakfasted in sunshine – back to one croissant, but two cups of coffee – and the early morning peacefulness of the Jardin des Plantes, soothed by birdsong. Normally, this had a calming influence on him; today, however, was the day of the commemoration that he'd attend, before going to the 'film-set' of the nearby café where he'd shape up and flesh out the final scene in his blueprint wherein the new lovers meet, and take whatever course they take – the continuum of Therese's and Bertrand's classic love story (in his head, he's dubbed it 'classic'), a scene both crucial and chancy, and one that he's apprehensive of his powers to create. It's on-the-edge time; will he – should he? – give his new characters their heads?

He paces the balcony, fingering his scar. Won't it depend on how they interpret the situation they're in, and what dialogue comes from each? Yet, in his view, it's a fallacy that characters take over and dictate to the author. The author always had final control. Should have. He'd be relying on the work that his unconscious had laid down. In his book *The Spooky Art*, Norman Mailer, a lesser mentor to him than Fowles, said: 'I take it for granted that my unconscious knows more than I do', and further, 'I discover that my unconscious is going to disclose to me what it chooses, when it chooses', and then, 'Perhaps, out of the corner of your eye, you glimpse someone in a restaurant who represents a particular impression or menace or possibility … and the unconscious goes to work on that'.

Pierre hadn't needed Mailer to tell him about the unconscious, but the dead American writer had given him pointers on how to manage it, to bring its blade-edge to the whetstone. In the case of this novel, the acid test of its potency would come when he finally sat down at his computer. From past experience, he was confident that it wouldn't let him down.

Last night, Lucile had phoned him; she'd said: 'Do you read *Paris Soir*?' 'No.' 'There was an article on the Cimetière du Père Lachaise, and your brigadier-general is mentioned …' She gave details, while he listened. 'There was a snippet, too, on television, but I suppose you didn't see that either.' I'm a researcher, she'd said before. He said, 'I know of the commemoration. It's tomorrow and I'm going.' Focus on the novel was everything to him now, and he didn't really wish to invite her to dinner, yet in the next breath he did, tomorrow night, at Monsieur Jacques' restaurant. The suave, well-tailored male companion with her the other night had flashed into his mind. Beyond the novel, he felt impelled to make an investment in the future and, unexpectedly, on the verge of putting black on white, he was. He realised how glad he was to be still figuring with her. He mused: Perhaps five years was enough time.

This morning, he'd put on a blue suit, pink shirt, silver tie, and laid the homburg and a black ebony cane on the hall table, in waiting. Madame Roget had observed these preparations with her circumspect eyes. He'd smiled; the tailor's dummy was making a sortie out to the city. He imagined that she thought along those lines. At least, he knew she liked to see him going out.

Brigadier-General Bertrand deserved better weather than this to mark his anniversary. It had begun to rain as Pierre left for the cemetery. He'd gone back to get a raincoat, and to exchange his cane for an umbrella that he now stood beneath, adjacent to the monument in one of the avenues of the Cimetière du Père Lachaise. Perhaps forty or so dedicated, sodden souls, also sheltering under black canopies, were clustered in the vicinity; a few less hardy, or less committed, had glanced about then hadn't waited for the ceremony.

A portly, florid-faced man blew a tremulous call on a cavalry trumpet resembling one of the stone-carved ones set into the monument; the nature of the call was unknown to Pierre (they hadn't gone in for bugle-work in the airborne). This individual was protected under a large, multi-coloured umbrella held aloft by a colleague. The trumpet notes struggled for crispness in the moisture-laden air.

All of this was a long way from the novelist's expectations: he'd had in mind a dreaming, sunlit occasion, with his thoughts coasting off through the trees, over the marble and masonry tombs and headstones, well-set on a creative journey.

When the last trumpet note had died out, a man, perhaps the president of what Pierre now realised was an obscure society, began to read in a hoarse voice from a script: Bertrand's dates, his decorations, his campaigns and battles, the regiments that he'd commanded, and mention of the twenty-one wounds that he'd suffered. Pierre smiled at that – was this the official count? He couldn't see the fellow's face under the multi-coloured umbrella held aloft over him, just heard the disembodied voice ticking the boxes of the general's life and career. It didn't last long, couldn't in the conditions, and before it was quite finished Pierre turned away and strode back to the gates. He walked, head lowered, watching his feet splash through the puddles, another call from the trumpet following him down the avenue. A depressing occasion. There'd been no mention of Therese, and through a gap in the huddled bodies he'd spied his six roses lying withered and desolate on the rain-washed marble of her tomb. Because of the forest of umbrellas, he hadn't been able to get a proper look at his companions.

He went to the nearby café.

Entering what had become – for his purposes, in his mind – the 'film-set', he shook the water from the umbrella, removed his raincoat and hat, and put them into a waiter's hands. He selected a corner table with a good view of the interior, and of a small terrace where chairs were upended on the tables. A dozen persons sat inside, and behind him a few others came trickling in for an early lunch. No Chambertin available here, and he chose a sauvignon blanc from the Loire, then studied the menu, decided to order a half-dozen of the oysters from Brittany; outside, near the door, in a stainless steel trough, he'd noted the huge oysters stacked on ice.

Pierre took a first sip of the wine and dismissed conscious thoughts: he'd have a run with Mailer; earlier this morning, under the cascading warmth of the rose-head shower, there'd been a preliminary jog. His new characters, hitherto, had been wandering in his mind like lost souls, but now he needed focus – to take hold of them, put flesh on them, breathe into them. From two as yet unnamed towns, they'd come to this commemoration connected to their forebears, which meant, he assumed, that they'd have a certain knowledge of family history – perhaps not much, but enough for their attention to be arrested when the national television item on the famous Paris cemetery, and the *France Soir* piece that Lucile had told him of, had mentioned the anniversaries of the deaths of two Napoleonic generals to be commemorated this month.

With the connivance of his Prince of Co-incidence, this was how Pierre had decided to bring the new lovers within range of each other: an unnamed man and woman, linked by a sabre and a shawl. He'd decided, in his mental blueprint, that respectively, they'd inherited those heirlooms. And the letters (there had to be letters) – the ones from Therese, the ones from Bertrand, that he'd been unable to discover. He'd not decided on their names, wished them to be right, and was waiting for his unconscious to pop them into his head. 'Nothing should be forced', he murmured. So here they were, but not soaked and sodden, he'd write it as a blazing blue, early summer's day.

The oysters were served, and hardly conscious of doing it, he took up one of the big midnight-blue shells and sucked down the coarse mollusc with a copious draught of its salt water … But what would be the catalyst for their face-to-face encounter? He nodded to himself. It'd be catch as catch can, when he sat down to write, meanwhile, it was marinating in his unconscious until the time arrived to pour it into the story, like a pitcher of whipped cream into a Montford-Lamaury tart. In a flicker of memory, that image came.

In the imagined perfect day, other images fretted in his brain, including sunlight and leaf-shadow on the cemetery path; scenes passed before his mind's eye as if they'd been pre-recorded on film and were being screened somewhere – maybe in a flea-house art cinema.

Itinerant thoughts, aplenty.

He ate more oysters, sipped the well-balanced Loire wine, felt that he was adrift in a productive zone (time will tell about that, he knows). Fragments were emerging into the light: the man is a retired bank manager, the woman a recently retired headmistress, both in their fifties, both single (divorced, widower or widow?), lonely individuals, leading shuttered lives; these imagined people nameless, and even faceless as yet, waiting to be lovers.

Pierre is breathing a little faster, he realises. Why so nervous? They're his characters to do his bidding, nothing beyond that; nevertheless, as always, there's the potential for that bidding to be a collection of false steps. In his heart, he knows that nothing is simple or easy. He heads for some safe ground: he'll send them to 'Chanson', together, let them wander around the ruin wondering and speculating, guessing from the letters they each have that it might be very significant, but without access to the saddle-maker's journal, unable to know how the ruin was once at the heart of their forebears' lives, and the *ménage à trois*, yet themselves falling under its lingering spell to – at this point – fall in love. Brakes! Too flamboyant – a sticky pastiche, going over the top. He takes a steadying and corrective sip of water, looks around, changes direction.

The tall woman, alone, with the striking auburn hair done up in a roll, her slender fingers on the stem of a wineglass, staring across the room, clearly lost in her thoughts could be his heroine from the unnamed provincial city. A smart-looking woman, the modern headmistress, detached from her girls, semi-reluctantly, looking for fresh fields – for love and companionship in her life – and dreaming of the Belgian shawl, of the morning's event. She sits in profile to him; the novelist studies her, trusting his unconscious to kick in and store away the image for further work. Good stuff. His eyes move on over other tables. Aha! The tall, thin fellow with the brown marks on his face, also alone, near the window, dolefully brooding on the rain-swept terrace, as if it's a metaphor for his life, could be his hero. The sabre is what's on his mind, held two hundred years ago in the hand of the man whose life and memory are honoured today. Pierre soaks in his appearance, his impressions on his provenance, and trusts that his unconscious is on this case, too. More good stuff … Both are about the right age. He thinks he has what he's seeking. They are actors who've strayed into the scene.

Pierre empties his glass, and signals for the bill. He doesn't want to stay too long in this mode, overdoing it; impressionistic is the ticket.

Dear Reader, pushy me again – I know you think that I'm a pain in the butt, as our American friends so basically say, but it's for the last time. In the narrative to date, such as it is, I've felt impelled to put a hand on the tiller now and then to keep Pierre on some kind of course. I'll be back when he sits down to write, but absolutely non-interventionist, no comments at all, as quiet and delicate in my omniscient character as Anton Brun's soft leather slippers shuffling in a 'Chanson' corridor at midnight – to use a trifle of this novelist's florid style. If you can stand it, another interloper is going to appear just for a few moments …

… Pierre is paying the bill, and does not glance up, nor does anyone else in the room, when the very large and overweight man appears in the café doorway, and, propped on a heavy walking stick, surveys the scene. He is dressed completely in black, a long macintosh down to his ankles, a fedora tilted forward so that the black curls on his neck are visible, and looks, I think, like the cash-strapped Orson Welles inspecting the abandoned and spooky Gare d'Orsay in the dawn light, realising that he's found the production-saving set for his most noteworthy film, *The Trial*. And he's just as he is in Pierre's dreams and imagination – his Prince of Imagination. Even if they had looked to the door, they'd have seen only the street with its steel-grey air and now misty rain. He looks in turn at Pierre, at the table with the auburn-haired woman, and the one with the skinny man, considers for a moment, nods to himself, turns and departs.

As I must; my landlord's threatening to put me into the street. Adieu.

Angelique thought: Thank heavens that man has gone! In the long mirror behind the bar that she faces, she'd seen his scrutiny of her profile from his nearby table. Intense scrutiny; it had an almost proprietary cast – not sexual attraction, though she was no expert on that, just very strange, and certainly mysterious. She sipped her wine; the glass still half-full. All of this day had a strange undercurrent, a fascinating strangeness. She was a woman of enthusiasms that were prized by her friends; her recent research into family history had been a marvellous stimulant, and today was a pinnacle. She'd loved the grey and dripping atmosphere as she'd stood at the tomb, the cracked trumpet notes – to her mind, a fitting cipher for the vanished empire, and emperor, and to her ancestor who'd lived in that world. And she'd loved the stonemason's modest but precise delicacy in her forebear's ethereal gravestone; she'd been right beside it, had been delighted yet unsurprised to find it here. 'Ethereal' was the word which always came into her mind in tandem with Therese; the portrait on her wall had etched that impression on her brain. Clearly, the artist of two centuries ago had, overwhelmingly, been convinced of it. She wondered who had laid down the six roses – also so precisely, like pieces of cutlery on a dining table. She looked into the Loire wine; felt that it had been a man. As she prepared to depart, she thought: Where do I go now; what comes next?

Henri ate his meal carefully, and with due consideration of what the chef had attempted, even in an establishment of this modest standard. Everything was relative, as with the unremarkable ceremony that he'd just witnessed; a tired, scrappy format, admittedly in difficult conditions, it reminded him of the rough cloth and cut, and the colour-faded uniforms, of the Emperor's regiments that he'd seen in glass cases in certain museums. No snap or vibrancy remained. But mainly, you should look beyond the physical to find a real essence of past times: into the air, the sky, and maybe the spiritual world. His accountant at the bank had been into the last – sitting around tables in darkened rooms, holding hands – but that wasn't what Henri had in mind. He was beginning to think that you could best find the past, and its inhabitants, in your own heart. Of course, Therese's letters had been fascinating. Her last to Bertrand was in his breast pocket.

He sipped pinot noir and meditated on the rain-shiny terrace and the water dripping from a vine-climbed pergola. The rain had stopped, pale traces of blue were appearing in the dissipating overcast. He should go soon. His thoughts of a moment ago had yielded nothing solid or useful. When he returned home, he'd take the sabre from its case, grip it and slash it through the air. That would be real, perhaps the closest he could get to the brigadier-general. He imagined a whistling sound: the song of the sabre sung on a lot of battlefields. For the first time that day, he grinned.

He'd thought that the ceremony might be an opportunity to meet distant relatives, but the conditions had prevented it, and it appeared that no one from the gathering had come to this café, though that was hard to determine. Nonetheless, he was glad he'd come. Hurrying back in the rain through the cemetery gates, while a Bartok sonata had been playing in his head, he'd seen this café – a port in a storm. Well, he was part of the history of Therese and Bertrand, wasn't he? And the desire to know more, in the abundance of leisure time now his, was growing in him; it seemed that his recent notion of being on the brink of a new step in his life actually meant something. So, what was the next step? He'd think about it on the return journey.

He paid the bill, and stood up to claim his raincoat and the umbrella that he'd bought on arrival this morning at the Gare de l'Est.

Angelique approached the café's front desk and asked for her raincoat and umbrella. The waiter went into a side room and brought out those articles.

She looked at them and said, 'No, those are not mine'.

A voice behind her said, 'I think they're mine'.

Angelique turned to look at the tall, thin man with a high forehead and sandy hair. He smiled at her, as the waiter pushed them into his hands, hurried back into the room and returned with Angelique's things.

'Bit confusing', Henri said. 'They're very similar.'

Later, she didn't know why she said it to a stranger, but she did: 'Confusing, or perhaps extraordinary is the kind of day I'm having'.

'Oh?', Henri studied the tall, elegant woman, with the striking auburn hair done in a style he admired. He took in her fine complexion, her provincial accent, the faint scent of her perfume. He couldn't disguise his intense scrutiny.

Not another one, Angelique thought, feeling her surprise. She didn't intend to say more. She put on the raincoat, straightened it, unfurled the umbrella, nodded to the man and the waiter, and left. An idea had come to her.

Henri put on his own coat as he watched her leave. Then he went out to the street. He looked to the right, then the left. The woman was entering the cemetery.

She stood beside Therese's gravestone, the sunlight now illuminating the marble dappled with raindrops.

'Excuse me', the same voice said, 'were you at the commemoration?'

She turned to face him. O God, she thought. Is it what I think it is? 'Yes, I was.'

'So was I. My name is Henri Brun.'

'I'm Angelique Verdier-Bertrand, this lady's descendant …' She nodded down at Therese's last resting place.

They looked at each other for a long moment, blue and green eyes connected in a wondering gaze, both minds trying to work out where they were, her thoughts moving faster than his, which on this occasion were not so precise, unable to grasp the veritable feast that might be ahead.

When Pierre came out to the Rue du Repos, passing the gurgling tub of oysters, it was misting with rain, which didn't worry him. Blue sky was appearing. He felt that it had been a productive morning: his characters now had physicality, no longer were faceless – each was photographed in his mind. Nonetheless, there was a lot more work to do. He'd decided how they would meet. Separately they'd leave the café, and go back through the cemetery gates to Bertrand's and Therese's graves; two people, with a common bond, gazing at the monuments, reading the inscriptions, not another soul present – except for the host of unseen ones. He grinned. Easy as pie … It would be the beginning of shared information, of long talks, of expeditions to various places to unearth, experience, more of their mutual heritage. He'd send them to Lille to dig into the saddle-maker's past, perhaps find his business and personal papers in a municipal archive. Maybe his fictional explorers would track him down at the saddle-maker's apartment, this cousin-novelist, who was writing their story. That'd be tricky, nonetheless … Certainly, he'd send them to 'Chanson'. Despite its ruinous condition, the old château would sing to them its song that had fascinated Anton Brun, and, under its spell, they'd fall in love! He gestured these outcomes to a patch of blue sky which had appeared like a window; and tonight, after his date with the green-eyed Lucile, who, more and more, was looming up in his mind's eye, somehow becoming integral with his novel, he'd sit down to begin the writing.

Monsieur Jacques, through the window of his cubby-hole, studied his eccentric novelist, sitting at the special corner table with the lady he'd brought to dinner, their faces aglow in the amber electric light. It was pleasing to see him with a woman again; the tall, dark, serious type, who'd been here before with another man. He'd been a little strange in recent weeks, he felt. Doing too much solitary.

Monsieur Jacques accepted his clientele as they were, so long as they didn't disturb the equilibrium of his establishment, but he took a closer interest in this novelist with the scar on his brow. He didn't read books, only newspapers, but he'd heard other patrons talking about him, and he knew of the tragedy in his life, his jail-time. He recalled some of his previous women: the red-haired investment banker, who'd talked shares, which had interested him – he'd nearly lost the restaurant twice from gambling on the exchange; finally, he'd made a right call and sold everything late in 2006, at near the top of the market, and, with relief, doused the gambling flame. To celebrate, his wife had bought him a silk dressing-gown. And he remembered the actress; a demanding, abrasive woman who one night had nearly given Franco, his oldest retainer, a heart-attack. He'd been at the point of asking Monsieur Brun not to bring her here again, when, thank God, she'd dropped out of his life, or been kicked out – a more satisfying possibility. As usual, Chambertin had been ordered; tonight, the novelist wouldn't need his company for one of the interesting toasts, and Monsieur Jacques was sure that there'd be one. None of his other patrons asked for this wine, and he'd checked that his stock was adequate: eight bottles.

Franco appeared in his window. 'Monsieur', he nodded towards Pierre, 'asks would you join him for a glass of wine'.

Pierre made the introductions and Monsieur Jacques bowed. 'It has been my pleasure to see Madame here on several occasions.'

Lucile smiled at him.

'Monsieur Jacques, please sit down and join us in a glass of your delicious wine … I have a rather special toast to propose … I am about to commence a novel.'

The restaurant proprietor smiled his congratulations, sat down and Franco poured a glass for him. Pierre looked into the ruby depths of his own glass, anticipating the taste of the pinot noir on his palate, considering words.

Evening breezes had swept aside the rain that had beset the city during the day, and the temperature had risen: summer was here. In celebration, Lucile had on a sleeveless silk frock and now he found himself staring, with fascination, at the constellation of marks on her arms. They were waiting. He looked again at the wine; they'd think him crazy, or at least play-acting, or tongue-in-cheek; none of that was the case. He was serious and sincere about this. He raised his glass, and they followed. 'To all the characters in my new novel, I wish them well.' They sipped the wine, and, with a bow, Monsieur Jacques withdrew, as usual, expressionless. Pierre speculated if he was holding back a smile. The speculation amused him.

'An interesting toast', Lucile said, almost to herself.

'With the Emperor's favourite wine', Pierre replied. And Anton's, he should have added.

He'd decided to tell her something more of the story than the little she knew, and beginning with today's events he did, speaking in a confidential tone, for five minutes or so.

When he stopped, she said, 'So you haven't written down a word?'

He nodded. 'These past weeks I've been living in another world – absorbing it.' He thought: And now I'm about to be sucked further into its depths. 'There's a blueprint in my head.'

They were silent while the dinner was served. She could imagine a lot of things with this man, and that might be part of the attraction that she felt. Nothing remotely similar had happened to her before. She gazes into her wine-glass, summing up her situation: he's self-absorbed, putting first those things which are first for him; offering no commitment. Doubtless, tonight's dinner invitation is meant to keep options open; how much time does he think he has? Neither of us has time to burn … Gazes at my arms as if he could eat them, into my eyes; does it mean anything? … She frowns. Clearly, the discovery of the journal, his forebear, has given him a big jolt, made him think about his life and the way ahead for what is left of it. Is that the way it is? She transfers her gaze to her dinner plate; they've left the meal to Paul, and she is looking at *filets de sole braisés au champagne* but has little appetite. She recalls the recipe that she'd asked the star chef for some weeks ago, which, when prepared, she'd had little appetite for either – like many of them, he'd left out a key ingredient, and she hadn't discovered what it was. And, one principal thing: though he might be unconscious of it, the wound of his wife's tragic death is still bleeding within him. There could be a slow healing over time; whichever way you turned, time was of the essence with this man. So? She looks at him, tells herself: *You really don't know, do you?* But this Chambertin, prized by his revered saddle-maker forebear, is delicious; this is Emperor's wine. Firmer ground.

As if at an appointed time in his life, Pierre sat at his desk in the shadowy but artistically lit salon, a spotlight directed onto his computer keyboard. The one compliment that the actress had ever paid him, though it was double-edged, came back: 'Maestro, the décor of this room is crap, but the lighting at night is beautiful'.

He turned in his chair, and regarded it. It seethed – no, perhaps a subtler tone than that – of history and its atmospheres, his family history, and its broader context. And the old garden, across the street, its bird-life slumbering in its bosom, could have been a nocturnal, botanical still-life. From the hall, the Sèvres clock that he assumed was a survivor of Anton's collection struck 10 p.m.

The opening sentences of the novel were in his head, but he was not quite ready. They were here, assembled in the salon that each knew so well – shadows in a crescent around his desk: his wife, his parents, the saddle-maker … a family affair. Again he turned in the chair, and glanced toward two dark corners at the end of the salon. And that's where *they'd* be, hopefully paying attention. He grinned in their direction.

He faced the keyboard, flexed his fingers. 'Okay, you eccentric, lugubrious cliché-lover, let's do it', he said, for the benefit of the watchers.

On a dark and stormy night in December 1804, at 5.55 p.m., the coachman, Marcel, guided the four chestnut mares and the berlin around the gravelled circuit to the front door of the château of 'Chanson'. He, and the two footmen perched on the back of the carriage, wore hats and black waterproofs. It wasn't raining yet, but in the heavens rumbling thunder was punctuated by sharp illuminations and whip-cracks of lightning; they had a two-hour journey before them to Reims, where the mayor was giving his annual ball.

Within the château's hall, servants waited with overcoats and umbrellas. Monsieur, very smart in a midnight-blue velvet jacket and white silk stockings, was already there, waiting patiently for Madame. He stared to the head of the stairs, his face serious but benign, in expectation of her imminent arrival. Despite contrary intimations, she was an efficient and punctual person. Then he smiled: here she was!

Madame paused at the top of the stairs, clearly for effect, and the women craning their necks emitted a collective, admiring 'Ooh!'

An instant manifestation of beauty, thought her husband Anton Brun, master saddle-maker and leather products-supplier to the Emperor's Grande Armée. She was descending now, one might say floating, in the ethereal wispy, grey and blue gown, the necklace of sapphires resplendent against her flawless throat and bosom; the same gown and necklace that she'd chosen for her recent portrait, he noted; her fine auburn hair, expertly dressed, was alive with shifting highlights, from the scores of candles flickering in the great hall.

'My dearest Therese, my angel', Brun said, starting forward, taking her hand and lifting it to his lips.

In a hurrying procession, they crossed the terrace to the berlin; the footmen were down, the steps in place, on the box Marcel touched his hat, and his patron waved a hand to him. Brun glanced up at the sky. Not yet raining, but at that moment more thunder rolled across the skies, as if out in the château's darkened park the massed drummers of the Imperial Guard were playing an ominous roll; with his military connections, he was increasingly using such analogies, and one such was especially appropriate on this night. The saddler-maker knew that an evening in the particular company they were travelling toward could be fraught with more peril for them than the storm presaged; nonetheless, he would take the rough with the smooth. He was allowing himself no other choice.

In the square at Reims, at 7.55 p.m., the thirty officers of the regiment of hussars temporarily quartered in the town were assembling prior to marching to the town hall across the square, where they were to be honoured guests at the mayor's ball. In full dress uniforms, with ceremonial swords, they were arriving in twos and threes from all directions, and being checked off a list by the adjutant. The younger ones were in high spirits, for a hussar loved action – whether in the ballroom, or on the field of battle. The colonel and the lieutenant-colonel were not yet present, but the adjutant, like a sheep-dog, now ordered them into a column, two by two, ready for the short procession.

Colonel Hubert Bertrand arrived at that juncture, glanced up at the sky where dark, low-flying clouds were racing above the town's steeples, and turned to cast an eye over his officers. 'Very well', he said to the lieutenant-colonel, who gave the order and the column set out across the square to the cheers and applause of the townsfolk.

A pharmacist, whose shop was on the square, stood amid fellow citizens with his fifteen-year-old son, both wrapped up to their throats. The boy's eyes were bright with interest and admiration, and the father smiled sadly. 'The uniforms!', the boy exclaimed. 'Father! It is a great honour to serve the Emperor!'

The pharmacist watched the column go in a leather-creaking, metal-jingling, heel-cracking cacophony. The very few older officers walked bow-legged and stiff. He thought: Wounds, and arthritis. The younger fellows had managed to grow the moustache, otherwise had the complexions of youths. The colonel would be in his forties, though looked older ... He said: 'Yes, very fine, as splendid as dragonflies, and with a life-span to match. A hussar does not live a long life, boy ...' He glanced aside at his son. 'Don't worry, the Emperor will send for you soon enough.'

The regiment's trumpeters, lined up at the town hall's door, now blew a fanfare.

At 8.15 p.m., the berlin arrived at the town hall and, in a flurry of attention from municipal servants, Monsieur and Madame Brun were ushered into the vast stone building.

Her hand on his arm, the saddle-maker could sense his wife's excitement. Their overcoats were taken from them in the vestibule, and the next moment they entered the hubbub of the crowded auditorium, ablaze with rainbow colours, the military men grouped like a tableau, the fiddles tuning up in the background. Glancing down at his wife, Anton Brun was moved to see her eyes shining, as if she were a child arriving at her first fairy party.

Later, Brun, the observer, hands behind his back, stood with two acquaintances, Messieurs Rey and Montmorency, who, like him were also ghost presences at these balls, and watched the colonel of hussars walking to where their wives were chatting while joyfully fluttering their exotic fans, and taking in the scene. A short, weathered fellow, in his late forties, but good-looking in a sober, serious way, the insignia of two famous orders on his breast, he came with the purpose and importance of a man on a mission for the Emperor. So thought the saddle-maker, who was becoming an expert on officers of the Grande Armée. The music began, to a shout of appreciation.

What then happened wasn't unexpected to Brun, though nonetheless it made him feel ill. The veteran came stiffly to attention before his wife, bowed, and gazed into her face and eyes, with what he imagined was the intensity of a long-distance stare across a smoky battlefield. A few words passed between them, Therese gestured slightly toward Brun, and the colonel was before him, bowing, introducing himself, requesting permission to dance with his wife.

The saddle-maker, looking steadily into the colonel's bright blue eyes, told himself: Anton, the rough with the smooth.

Pierre looks up from his keyboard; abruptly, the salon is alive with the fluttering and rustling of fabrics and papers, as if the lung that is the Jardin des Plantes has exhaled a breath in anticipation of the new day's arrival. He glances at his watch, a few seconds past midnight – midnight in Paris. The figures that he imagined and sensed present earlier have stepped into the darkness at the back of his mind, into his unconscious.

He looks down at the screen. He's begun, and the narrative from Anton's journal, with his own variations, will take him deep into the story, then the continuum of the classic love affair will take him on – who knows where; he guesses that bits and pieces of it could wander off the edge of the page, and he trusts that the more intrepid and imaginative readers might follow.

In his right ear, Fowles says, again: 'One of the greatest arts of the novel is omission – leaving it to the reader's imagination to do the work'. In his left ear, Mailer says: 'Trust your unconscious'. Well, he does, and it's where his two fanciful princes will be in touch. Hopefully.

One other thing: his agent has written, pleading ill-health, informing him that his publisher's been in contact saying that, after five years, they hear on the grapevine (Lucile? is she a fifth columnist?) that he's working on a new novel, reminding them that a last title is overdue on his contract, and hoping to hear about this, otherwise … He grins. Otherwise? Water off a duck's back. A final thing: it seems to him that he's stepped out of the cage he's been in for five years; there is still a long journey ahead, but it will be travelled with a warmer heart. He slips back into 1804, begins to type the next sentence in his 'lugubrious' – as the critic said – prose. He'll have to watch this. But will he?